Hannah

Silicon Valley Billionaires, Book 3

By Leigh James

Copyright © 2018 by Leigh James.

ISBN: 978-1945340161

Published by Jack's House Publishing, LLC

Cover by Kristina Brinton and Ashley Lopez

Sign up for Leigh's mailing list at www.leighjamesbooks.com.

This is a work of fiction. Names, characters, and incidents either are the product of the author's imagination or are used fictitiously, and any resemblance to actual persons, living or dead, business establishments, events, or locales is entirely coincidental.

Chapter 1

HANNAH

"Hey." I carefully nudged Wes's shoulder, and he groaned.

He pulled me against his chest. "Hey what?"

I nestled against his big body, warm underneath the blankets, while staying mindful of his bandages—and the wounds they protected. "I have to get up. Today's the day!"

He pulled me closer, grinning. The early morning sun bathed his handsome face and square jaw; his crew cut glinted in the light. "I know. I'm excited for you."

"Thanks." I kissed him, desire zipping through me as our tongues connected, his hands flexing against my hips. Now *I* was the excited one. My skin flushed with heat—I wanted him. *Bad.*

So I hastily pulled back and scooted away.

Wes reached for me.

"Easy, stud," I mock scolded him. "Dr. Kim said you need to take it slow, and I'm not going against doctor's orders."

"Aw, baby, come back."

I grabbed his hand and kissed it. "Trust me, I want to. But we have to behave."

Wes frowned, but his eyes sparkled good-naturedly. "Buzzkill."

I giggled and hopped out of bed. Maybe I *was* a buzzkill, but rules were rules. The doctor said we should abstain for a few more weeks, to be sure Wesley's heart was strong enough for…you know.

His heart. I shivered, remembering the night they had shot him right in front of me. I'd watched him go down. I'd thought he was dead…

"I'll be back in a minute, okay?" I kept my tone upbeat and blew him a kiss.

"I won't get too far." He winked.

He was making a joke, but guilt still shot through me as I headed from our wing in Gabe and Lauren's house to their massive kitchen. Wes was recovering from a gunshot wound, a head injury, and a medically induced coma—all earned while he'd been protecting me on assignment.

So much had happened in such a short time; I got whiplash just thinking about it. Before all the craziness—*just a few short weeks ago!*—Wes and I had been in hot and heavy infatuation mode. When we had plans, I'd dress up, spending so much time on my makeup and hair, you'd think I was headed for the red carpet. I wore lingerie, anticipation zinging through me, just waiting to be with him.

Now we were living with my sister and her fiancé because I couldn't bear to stay in the house where we'd been attacked. Wes was here because he needed help getting around. We were medically forbidden to have sex. We shared a bathroom. He'd seen me in my sweats with no makeup on. He'd seen me in a *mud mask*.

I wasn't sure what to make of any of this.

We'd gone from causally dating to almost dying to living together. And although I considered myself a hardcore type A, who always had a master plan and a checklist, I had no idea what came next.

I checked my phone as I hustled to the kitchen. But as the screen lit up, I stopped in my tracks. There were five frantic texts from my longtime friend, Fiona Pace.

I have a situation I need to talk to you about.

Are you up yet? Text me when you can.

I'm worried about Protocol Therapeutics…

Is there any way we can meet today?

Can you please text me? I'm about to lose it.

I read and re-read the messages, my heart pounding. *What's going on?* I wrote.

Fiona responded immediately. *Getting girls ready for school now. I'll call you in a little bit. I need to see you and Lauren today, if possible.*

Okay, I wrote back. But I didn't feel okay.

I made it to the kitchen and grabbed a much-needed coffee, my mind whirling. I'd known Fiona for years, but I'd *never* seen her stressed. If I was a type A, Fiona was a Triple A. She was a Silicon Valley legend. She managed hostile corporate takeovers and multibillion-dollar IPOs—all while juggling her family, charitable commitments, and TED talks—without breaking a sweat or smudging her lip gloss.

We were good friends, but I hadn't spoken to her recently. Things had been so intense with our company's release of its revolutionary health patch and the crazy surrounding circumstances—including Wes being shot, let alone my kidnapping and being held hostage—that there hadn't been much time to chat.

I thought about her texts as I grabbed my coffee, hustling back to take a quick shower. What had Fiona so rattled? In her latest corporate incarnation, she was the all-star CEO of Protocol Therapeutics, a hot new start-up that had the industry buzzing with speculation about its enormous valuation. Reportedly, Protocol was developing a cancer antibody therapy. If it worked, it was going to revolutionize healthcare.

Technology like this could change the world.

I got out of the shower in record time, toweled off, and hastily blow-dried my hair, scrolling through Protocol Therapeutics's website on my phone. Fiona had assembled an all-female leadership team, which was no small feat in male-dominated Silicon Valley.

Why is she worried about her company?

There had to be an excellent reason. I shivered, bracing myself. I needed to find out what it was.

***

I fidgeted on my way into Paragon, the groundbreaking Silicon Valley biotechnology company my sister had started years ago. I kept expecting Fiona to call, but she didn't.

To stay occupied, I texted Marcus, the nurse I'd hired—just to check in on Wes. I texted him again when I got to my desk. I texted him ten minutes later to remind him that Wes liked the special electrolyte-enriched bottled water in the fridge. Then I texted him again to make sure he'd received my text.

Finally, Wes himself texted me: *Chill out and please stop driving Marcus crazy.*

Fine, I texted back, *but make sure he gets you the right water, and don't forget the sandwich I made you is in the fridge!*

I felt guilty for leaving him, but the feeling was nothing new. Guilt had been my BFF for the past few weeks. What had happened was my fault—Li Na Zhao, the Chinese corporate terrorist extraordinaire, was after me and my sister, Lauren, CEO of Paragon. Wes had been shot protecting me. The night Li Na's men ambushed us in my kitchen, I'd been distracting him, flirting and making a joke. We weren't paying attention. They shot the guards outside my house first, and we never even heard them. That was on *me.* They shot Wes, and he almost died, and that was also on *me.* And although he'd been home from the hospital for five weeks and I hadn't left his side, the guilt refused to leave me.

Sometimes I wondered if it ever would.

Still, it felt good to be back in my sunny, cheerful office. When I'd been held captive, I'd wondered if I'd ever sit at my desk again… I pushed the thought from my mind and plowed through our most recent sales data, checking my phone every three seconds.

Still no Fiona.

The good news was that I had plenty of work to distract me. The patch, Paragon's hit technology, continued to surpass all sales projections. As director of publicity, I needed to share this news with the world, so I started drafting a long-overdue press release.

My phone buzzed, and I jumped, even though I'd been waiting for it.

"Hannah? It's Fiona."

"How are you?"

"Not good," she said immediately. "And unfortunately, you're going to understand why all too well."

My stomach dropped. "Wh-what does that mean?"

"I'd rather not talk about it over the phone. Can I come up? Can I meet with you and Lauren right now?"

"You're *here*?"

"I'm in the parking lot. I was hoping you could fit me in—it's important."

"Hold on. Let me text Lauren and see if she's free."

I put her on hold and fired off a quick text to Lauren, the hair on the back of my neck standing up. Fiona worked sixteen-hour days and didn't waste time—ever. Sitting in a parking lot hoping for a meeting was *not* her style.

I read the reply from Lauren and got back on the phone with Fiona. "We can see you, but it needs to be quick. Lauren's due back in the lab in a half hour."

"That's fine. I'm coming in now."

My sister jumped to her feet when I came in. "What does Fiona Pace want? I'm so busy today. There's so much catching up to do—"

"I don't know, but she sounded upset. And Fiona doesn't do upset."

"I don't like it." Lauren shook her head, her blonde hair tumbling over her shoulders. "I have a bad feeling about this."

I did, too, but I didn't want to say it.

Stephanie, Lauren's longtime assistant, buzzed her in. "Ms. Pace is here."

"We're ready for her."

Fiona came through the doors wearing a violet sweater and a pencil skirt, her brown bob shining in the sun that streamed through the windows. She would've looked fabulous if her face hadn't been so tense. "Lauren, Hannah, thank you for seeing me on such short notice."

"It's a pleasure to meet you, Fiona," Lauren said. "It seems like Protocol Therapeutics is doing well—congratulations."

"Thank you, that means a lot." Fiona turned and pulled me in for a hug. "It's so good to see you."

I hugged her back, hard. "What's going on?"

Fiona smiled, but anxiety rolled off her in waves. "I'll tell you everything, but first—I've been worried sick. How are you?"

News of my kidnapping and the shooting at my house had been covered by the local press. Lauren and her attorney, Bethany O'Donnell, had done their best to keep the spotlight off Paragon and its violent entanglement with Jiàn Innovations, the Chinese biomedical giant that had tried repeatedly to steal our invention. But people in the industry still talked.

Fiona sank into the nearest seat. "We've all been praying for you—me, Jim, and the girls. I'm so sorry about what you've been through. What a nightmare."

"Thank you. But I'm fine, and I'm thrilled to be back at work. Tell us what's going on, because now I'm worried about *you*."

Fiona played with her rings. "Things are going well at Protocol—*very* well. We're getting close with the antibody therapy, and I think it's going to work. This could be big, a bigger innovation than we've seen in biotech in a long time. With the exception of your patch, of course."

Lauren smiled. "Thank you."

"That's amazing news." I leaned forward. "So why're you so upset?"

Fiona raised her gaze to meet mine, and I saw how hollowed-out she looked. "Because Li Na Zhao wants to steal the technology from me. And for the first time in my adult life, I'm scared. Scared, as in totally fucking petrified."

Chapter 2

HANNAH

Lauren put her face in her hands while I sat there, reeling.

"Why do you think it's Li Na?" My voice sounded hoarse.

Fiona sighed. "Because she called me, right after my IT team caught her trying to hack into our server."

Lauren looked up. "What did she say?"

"That Jiàn Innovations was interested in acquiring Protocol. When I explained we weren't selling, she wasn't too happy."

"Did she threaten you?" I asked.

Fiona shifted in her seat, as if talking about Li Na caused her physical discomfort. "Not exactly. In other words, she didn't say anything specific enough that I could take to the police or the FBI. But she *did* say that if I didn't reconsider, I'd regret it."

Lauren and I locked eyes for a moment, but neither of us said anything.

"Listen, people in Silicon Valley talk," Fiona said. "You haven't gone public with what happened, but I'm aware that Jiàn Innovations has been after Paragon. I also know that your former board member Clive Warren got involved with Jiàn when he was in China, and that he brought that shit-show home with him when he came back to California."

Fiona pursed her lips. "I'm not here to put you in another bad position—I'm just wondering if you have some insight on how to deal with her. I've been hacked at every company I've ever been with, but I've never been directly threatened like this. And after what happened with Hannah, my concerns have escalated. That's why I wanted to meet with you."

"I hate to say it, but you're right to be scared." Lauren pulled out a business card from her desk drawer. "You should contact the FBI—they'll want to know about this immediately. I've worked with Agent Marks. He's in charge of Li Na's file, which is getting thicker by the minute."

Fiona accepted the card Lauren, turning it over in her fingers. "Can he actually do anything?"

"Unfortunately, not much." Lauren frowned. "The United States has limited jurisdiction—we can't just arrest a Chinese national on Chinese soil, and as far as we know, her government has no plans to extradite her."

Fiona nodded. "That's pretty much what my attorney said."

"You should increase your security immediately. Li Na's holed up in Shenzhen, but that doesn't mean she isn't active over here. She has a pretty extensive team of thugs waiting to do her bidding." I shivered, hoping Lauren wouldn't notice.

She leaned forward, watching my face. "Hannah? Are you okay?"

Of course, my nosy big sister didn't miss a trick. "I'm fine. Please, we've got bigger problems right now—like the fact that Li Na's using these tactics again on another American biotech company. She's not backing down at all."

Apparently, a trail of dead guards and a botched buyout weren't enough to deter her.

I trained my gaze on Fiona. "Like I said, you need to increase security at work *and* at home. Li Na means business. She fights dirty."

Fiona continued to turn Agent Marks's card over in her hands. "I've never had security before. Personal security, I mean."

"The brothers of Lauren's fiancé run a security company. They're excellent. Would you like me to have them get in touch?" I asked.

"No, it's fine. You've already helped me enough. My attorney recommended a firm, I just haven't contacted them yet."

"You should," I said. "Today."

"I know. I just keep hoping that she's going to be reasonable, or the authorities in Shenzhen are going to do something about her."

Lauren shook her head. "The authorities have been useless. You have to expect the worst."

I grabbed my phone and shared Levi's contact information with Fiona. "Your attorney might know a great firm, but Betts Security is the best, and they've already dealt with Li Na. Call them as soon as you leave here."

Fiona pinched the bridge of her nose as if to ward off a headache. "I can't believe we're talking about this. Protocol is just wrapping up successful clinical trials. Our therapy could literally help *millions* of sick people—and then this bitch shows up again."

"It *is* a shock." Lauren kept her tone gentle. "Both of our companies are trying to do good work that will help people. It's unnerving that someone would try to steal it, but this might be the new normal. Tech is like the Wild West. Li Na Zhao wants to take over the biotech marketplace and she wants to establish Shenzhen as the international hub of innovation—and she's not waiting for permission."

"Jiàn Innovations has had some success, but it's on a small scale compared to what you and Lauren are doing," I said. "Small isn't good enough for Li Na. She wants more, and she wants it *now*. Clearly, she's not above stealing—in fact, now that she's approached you, too, I think she views it as the most expedient way to conduct business."

Fiona looked stricken. "Jesus."

Lauren sat back. "Call the FBI."

"And Levi Betts." I nodded at Fiona. "Trust me, you can't take too many precautions in this situation. Please stay in touch with us. We've been there—you're not alone."

"I'm sorry to involve you, but I just didn't know what else to do." Fiona stood to go.

I stood, too, and pulled my friend in for one last hug. "Don't be sorry. Be *careful*."

But as I watched her leave, I was still worried. As my sister and I had learned the hard way, when it came to Li Na Zhao, careful wasn't close to good enough.

* * *

I let the office early, which was unheard of in Silicon Valley—but I was anxious to get home to Wes. The whole ride, my mind worried over Fiona's story. It had only been a few weeks since Gabe and the Betts security team had rescued me and shot multiple members of Li Na's team, killing three men. But Li Na hadn't even hit the pause button, already trying to hack into another California company and threatening its CEO the same way she'd threatened Lauren.

By the time the driver pulled up to the gate at Gabe's compound, my palms were sweaty and I had a headache.

Brian, one of the three personal security agents assigned to me, noticed. He peered at me. "Are you okay, Ms. Taylor? You look a little pale."

"Ms. Taylor is my sister—so *please* call me Hannah—and yes, I'm fine. It was my first day back at work, though, and it felt like a long time to be away from Wesley." And the house. I breathed a sigh of relief as we went inside, grateful for the security of the familiar surroundings and also, the quiet.

Wes and Marcus, the handsome, dark-skinned, silver-haired nurse, were in the kitchen. Wes was standing, something he was approved to do only under supervision and in relatively short spurts.

I went and carefully wrapped my arms around him. I sighed in relief as I pressed my face against his chest, feeling his muscles surround me. I inhaled, relishing his familiar scent—a mixture of something manly (and testosterone-y) and clean laundry. *Yum.* "Hi."

"Hey, babe. You're home earlier than I expected."

I leaned up on my tiptoes and kissed his nose. "I missed you. Seven hours away was long enough."

Wes grinned, causing a familiar tug in my belly.

"It's good to see you." He took my face in his hands, his lips hungrily meeting mine. I wrapped my arms around his neck, clinging to him and molding my body against his. Our tongues connected, and I almost moaned. Luckily, I remembered myself…and all the other people in the room.

We pulled apart, Wes giving me the crooked grin I loved. "Oops." But he didn't sound sorry. The erection straining out toward me didn't look too apologetic, either.

The guards busied themselves rechecking the interior of the house, and Marcus scooted down the hallway toward the entryway. He turned to wink at us, clearly amused. "I'll just grab my stuff and get going."

Wes waved. "Uh…thanks."

He smiled. "See you in the morning."

Wes turned back to me, cheeks heated. "I won't be able to look Marcus in the eye tomorrow."

"Ugh, I'm sorry."

He laughed and pulled me back against his chest. "Don't you dare apologize—I just can't wait to get you alone."

I jerked my head toward the four security guards in the living room, all deferentially facing away and probably silently laughing their asses off. "Would you like to go outside and get some fresh air?"

"That'd be great."

"You have to, *you know*."

I motioned to the wheelchair, and Wes cursed under his breath. "I am so over that thing."

"Please? You won't have to use it for too much longer." Dr. Kim had said that he'd need it for only a few weeks, until Wes had progressed with physical therapy and gotten stronger.

He sank begrudgingly into the chair, arranging his large body and looking uncomfortable, a jaguar in a too-small cage. He rarely complained, but when he did, it was about not being able to get around by himself.

"I'm sure it's getting old."

Wes rolled his eyes. "Try ancient."

I didn't blame Wes for losing patience—he wasn't a sideline kind of guy. He liked working out. He liked being strong. He liked protecting me. He *hated* that he was missing work, just like he hated being stuck in this chair.

Speaking of things he hated… I swallowed nervously as I maneuvered him outside. He was going to freak about Li Na Zhao's sudden reappearance. I didn't want to stress him, but I *had* to tell him.

She'd put him in this chair. He deserved to know the truth.

"So, some stuff happened at Paragon today," I explained as we headed for the pool deck.

Wes went instantly on alert. "What kind of stuff?"

"Fiona Pace, the Protocol Therapeutics CEO, stopped by. She's a friend of mine, but this wasn't a social visit."

"The women-in-business leadership guru? I read her book. I thought it was great."

I stopped the chair and peered down at him, dumbfounded. *Wes read her book?* Fiona had written a bestseller about women in business, but it'd never crossed my mind that he'd pick something like that up. "You did?"

He chuckled at my expression. "Yeah, back when I started dating you. I thought it would give me insight."

"Insight on what?"

"On how to respectfully interact with a high-powered professional woman."

My heart swelled, touched by his preparation. "You thought of me as a high-powered professional?"

"I *think* of you as a high-powered professional."

I pulled the wheelchair up next to the chaise lounges. "That's sort of hot."

Wes tilted his chin, inspecting me. "You're hot—and you're totally high powered. Sometimes I don't think you see yourself clearly, babe."

"Oh. I guess I don't really think about it." I was used to Lauren always getting the professional attention and accolades.

I started to help Wes from the wheelchair to a chaise, but he gave me a very pointed look, so I backed off. I bit my lip as he used his arms, lifting himself. He winced a little, and my heart broke, but I looked away. Wesley didn't want my pity—in the weeks since the shooting, I'd at least figured that much out.

He settled himself onto the chair with some effort, then sighed. "Tell me more about Fiona Pace."

I sat down next to him. "It isn't good news. She's been the CEO of Protocol Therapeutics for about two years. They're researching antibody therapies to help cancer patients."

"Right, I've read about them."

My brow furrowed. "You have?"

"Of course—their valuation came in at seven billion dollars. Not bad for a company that hasn't even completed clinical trials yet."

When he saw the shocked look on my face, Wes laughed. "I can actually read at grade level, you know. I can even do it when I make a muscle at the same time." He winked.

"I know—of course I knew that." But my cheeks burned. *I'd underestimated him, and I just got busted.*

I cleared my throat and continued. "Fiona's IT team realized they were being hacked recently. They changed their firewalls so the person couldn't get in."

Wes frowned. "I'm waiting for the part where the news gets bad, and I'm dreading it."

I blew out a deep breath. "It's Li Na—she called Fiona and told her that since she can't hack in, she wants to outright buy Protocol."

Wes's face hardened. "And?"

"And when Fiona refused, Li Na threatened her."

Silence stretched out between us as he processed the news.

Wes finally shook his head, looking as if he'd like to crush something. "Jesus. She didn't even take a breather."

"I know. Lauren and I told Fiona to call the FBI, and we gave her Levi's number. She's supposed to call him today."

"Unfuckingbelievable." Wes stared straight ahead, his jaw taut. "It's time."

"Time for what?"

"To take Li Na *out*. She's done enough damage—we can't let her get away with any more. I'm done with waiting."

My heart thundered, and I reached for him, panicked. "The FBI will handle it."

He wrapped his arms around me, cradling me carefully to his chest. "They haven't managed to handle it yet, babe."

"I know, but they'll do something this time. She can't just keep getting away with *murder*."

Wes played with my hair. "You're right about that."

I pulled back, my gaze zeroing in on his. "It can't be you. I need you."

Wes chuckled. "You didn't even know I could read until two minutes ago."

"I didn't mean it like that—" I spluttered.

He put his finger over my lips, shushing me. "I'm just teasing you, honey."

I tried to relax against him, but the panic wouldn't recede. "Just promise me."

"Promise you what?"

"That you'll stay safe. That you'll stay with *me*."

Suddenly I wished I had that master plan and checklist, because I didn't even know what I was asking for. Still, I nestled against Wes, needing his assurance.

But although he continued to hold me, he never answered.

Chapter 3

WES

Li Na Zhao is back. I swear to God, I am going to gut her, once and for all…

I wasn't in shape to go after her yet, but I vowed to get ready. Then I tried desperately to think about something else so I would talk about something else. I didn't want to push poor Hannah over the edge. She'd been through enough already.

Because of Li Na.

My hands curled into fists, but I pushed the thoughts from my mind.

I played with Hannah's hair as we sat outside, not talking. Scrambling for something to say to break the tension, I sat up a little. "Hey, I forgot—I have a surprise for you."

She perked up immediately, blue eyes sparkling in what was left of the sun. "What?"

"C'mon, let's go back to the house. It's just a little something." I just wanted to show her that I appreciated her and everything she'd been doing for me for the past few weeks. She'd been taking care of me like she was family.

She was starting to *feel* like family, too, which scared the hell out of me. When I'd started working at Paragon, there'd been a string of different men, mostly sporting trendy beards and collarless leather jackets, showing up like clockwork in their Range Rovers to whisk Hannah out to lunch or dinner at various Silicon Valley hotspots. I never saw her go out with the same guy twice.

Things had been going good with us before the attack—*so* good. But we were in uncharted territory, my defunct ass was living in her sister's house, and Hannah was stuck waiting on me…

I got back in the godforsaken chair, vowing to get rid of it ASAP. I'd just have to push it harder in physical therapy.

Hannah wheeled me through the house, toward our wing.

"We're heading to our room for a while," I told the guards.

"No problem." Brian nodded. "We got you covered."

"Don't you think living with all these guys is sort of weird?" Hannah asked, keeping her voice low as we maneuvered through the long hallway to our suite, located on the western side of the house.

"No, but that's because I was in the military. And because my brother's been my roommate forever." A Special Ops marine, my brother Ellis wasn't home much because he'd been deployed overseas, but that was about to change.

"Will he be home soon?"

"Yeah. He's officially retiring from the service—I still can't believe it. He's going to start working for Betts Security at the beginning of the month."

Levi Betts and Ellis had gotten friendly while my brother had been home, visiting me in the hospital. Ellis had over a decade of experience with the Special Forces, and Levi had jumped at the chance to bring him onto his security team. Ellis had been thankful for the opportunity, but I still couldn't believe he was leaving the military.

"Are you excited he's moving home?"

I shrugged. The topic made me uncomfortable. "I have mixed feelings about it."

"Why?"

"Because I feel like he's giving up his career for me. He said he didn't want to be so far away anymore, after what happened. But I'm *fine*."

"Wes." Hannah stopped pushing my chair and came alongside me. "He misses you and wants to be closer. I'm sure he was scared to death when you got hurt—but you shouldn't feel guilty. He loves you and just wants to be here for you."

"I know that, but leaving the service is pretty extreme. Ellis is all military—I honestly can't even picture him as a civilian. I don't even know what he's going to do with himself."

"Levi will keep him busy. He said their business is growing exponentially because all the tech CEOs in Northern California want to increase security."

"I know, and that's good. But I don't think Ellis has taken a weekend off in ten years."

"He doesn't have a girlfriend or anything?" Hannah asked.

"*Hell* no. I don't think he's ever had a real relationship. There've been plenty of girls, but no one he ever brought home."

"Well, maybe he'll find a worthy candidate in Silicon Valley."

"Maybe." I couldn't picture Ellis taking a woman out to dinner and a movie. All he normally did with his free time was clean his guns and drink beer.

"I think he will." Hannah, ever the optimist, seemed determined.

"I'm going to have to buy a new house," I complained. "There's no way I could live with him full-time. I love him, but he drives me nuts."

"You don't need to buy a new house right now. We're staying here where it's safe, remember?"

We got to our suite, and I held my breath as she opened the door. With Marcus's help, I'd filled the room with flowers and flickering candles.

Hannah turned to me, eyes shining. "Wesley, what did you do?"

I grinned. "I wanted to celebrate you going back to work."

She walked around the room, examining the flowers. "Oh. Wow." She hugged her arms around herself, suddenly looking like she might cry.

"Hey—come here."

She came over, and there *were* tears in her eyes.

"I didn't mean to make you cry. I'm happy for you."

Her tears spilled over. "I'm happy, too."

She wiped her eyes, leaning down to kiss me. I cupped her face in my hands, wishing to Christ I could sweep her off her feet and carry her to the bed. Our tongues tangled, and I pulled her gently onto my lap. She felt my erection and scooted off me, breaking our embrace.

"Honey, we can't do this."

I pointed at my dick. "It doesn't have to be involved *at all*. This is about you."

She closed her eyes and shook her head. "Let's just wait, okay? Until we can both participate? I wouldn't feel right about it."

"You don't want to let me touch you?"

Hannah's face fell. "Of course I do. But it wouldn't be the same—I don't want it to be all about me."

I smiled at her gently. "I am more than prepared for it to be all about you. But if you don't want to do this right now, I understand."

Still, something about her reaction bothered me. This wasn't the first time since I'd been out of the hospital that she'd avoided getting physical. I didn't know if it was because she was worried she'd hurt me, wasn't as attracted to me in my beat-up state, or if it was something else…the same something she'd had a nightmare about last night. She'd woken up screaming for the third night in a row.

Looking crushed, Hannah reached for my hand. "I'm not *rejecting* you. You know that, right?"

"Of course." But it sounded like a lie.

She ran her hands through my hair, her wide blue eyes looking at me with concern. "I can't *wait* to be with you again. Seriously, I think about it all the time. But I don't think I'd be able to relax if I'm the only one getting naked. And you've already done so much"—she motioned around the room to the candles and the flowers—"in addition to taking a bullet for me. I don't want to be a taker."

I laughed. "You're kidding, right? You moved me into your sister's house, and you've been waiting on me hand and foot. If anyone's a taker, it's me."

We looked at each other for a beat, neither of us sure how to proceed.

"Do you want to…have an antioxidant smoothie and watch the draft on ESPN?"

She patted the bed, looking at me hopefully.

The draft sounded promising. But the smoothie, which would be filled with kale and some weird green powder that Hannah insisted was good for me, was a tougher sell. Still, I forced myself to smile. "With you? You know it."

That was one thing I'd realized over the past few weeks: I couldn't say no to her. Ever. Even though kale was bitter. Even though she'd probably suggest tofu for dinner, when all I wanted was a big, juicy steak.

Even though she wanted me to stay put, and not kick Li Na Zhao's ass.

I couldn't say no to her. But I desperately wanted to say *yes* to some ass-kicking.

* * *

Hannah curled up against me and I played with her long, thick hair as we watched ESPN.

At one point she sat up and stretched. "We should probably go have dinner, and check in with Lauren and Gabe. And I need to call Fiona."

"Okay." I started to sit up, but she stopped me with a kiss—long and deep. It made me yearn for her to be closer.

"Let's go in a minute." Her voice was husky. She kissed me again, our tongues connecting, and she pressed herself against me.

Of course, I got instantly hard, but I pulled back, not wanting to freak her out.

"What's wrong?" she asked.

I pointed at myself, sighing. "It's my dick. It's hard again."

She giggled. "Um, I'm right here—I *know*."

I willed it to go down.

She tilted her head, watching me. "Are you okay?"

"Yeah, of course. I just don't want you to be upset."

"Honey, I'm not upset." She reached out and stroked my face. "I mean, I *do* get upset that you're hurt. And I also know you're frustrated right now because you can't do all the things you normally do. Like…me."

We both laughed, breaking the tension a little.

I shrugged. "It's my issue, and I'm handling it."

"It's *our* issue. I don't want you to resent me."

She didn't say it, but there was an unspoken *resent me more than you already do* hanging around, invisible but palpable.

I laced my fingers through hers. "I could never resent you."

She sighed. "I don't see why not—you *did* get shot because of me. And get put in a medically induced coma. And now you're being forced to use a wheelchair that you hate."

I straightened. "Babe, we've had this conversation. I'm over it. I was shot on assignment, and it was part of my job. Even if it wasn't, I would have done anything I could to protect you. Because that's my *real* job. And if I remember correctly, I failed. You still got kidnapped…the other guards were shot…" I cut myself off. I couldn't bear to think about that night, about the friends I'd lost.

Hannah bit her lip, as if attempting to keep her objections inside.

"So—you feel guilty, I feel guilty." I squeezed her hand, trying to stay in the moment. "I think we're even."

There was a knock on the door, and we both jumped.

"Hannah?" Lauren called from the other side of the door. "Can you come out here? I need to talk to you—there's something going on at Paragon."

Hannah sprang from the bed, opening the door. "What is it?"

I caught a glimpse of Lauren's pale face. "It's bad."

I didn't have to hear more. I felt it in my gut. *Li Na's back—and she's not taking no for an answer.*

That was fine by me. This time, I'd be ready. This time, I'd keep Hannah safe. This time, I'd end it.

Chapter 4

LI NA

People, even smart people, fail to recognize the finite nature of time. There are limits. The limits need to be observed carefully, because otherwise, one day you'll wake up old and blindsided, on the other side of a life that had no meaning.

I'd gotten married in my twenties because my parents expected me to. Before I blinked, I'd wasted ten years trying to figure out if my husband was happy with me or not. Then I woke up one morning and realized I didn't care. Why should I? My husband had been a distraction, something I put in my own way to keep myself from my true potential. I would never get those ten years back. Ten years of dinners. Ten years of leaving the office to go home. Ten years of being a dutiful wife and daughter.

Such a waste.

I stood at my desk, examining the latest testing results from Protocol Therapeutics. But my thoughts kept going back to those ten years. I hated it when my mind wandered, but I'd noticed it did so for a reason, connecting dots I'd assumed were unrelated.

When I'd gotten divorced, I moved to an apartment. I bought a coffeemaker, a couch, and a bed, knowing guests and entertaining wouldn't be an issue. My parents were dead. My husband had remarried. I didn't bother socializing with friends—I just got to work.

It was the happiest I'd ever been.

Cutting things out of my life, even things that others deemed important, like relationships, remained one of the smartest things I'd ever done. I'd acted like a heart surgeon with a scalpel, trimming the unwanted growth from my heart. All that remained was me. Me and my commitment.

I pulled up Protocol's website. The remarkable people at the company had developed a groundbreaking antibody therapy to treat cancer. The technology was amazing, faster and more promising than anything that had come before it. The problem, as I saw it, was Protocol's CEO, Fiona Pace. Her vision remained too narrow. She was bending over backward conducting clinical trials, when the reports from the last round conclusively showed the technology worked.

What Fiona Pace didn't realize was the same thing Lauren Taylor hadn't realized: time waits for no one. Ultimately, I was on their side. I might not be able to organically recreate the level of innovation either woman had achieved, but I had the vision and the international business acumen to bring each of their technologies to full realization. I planned to take over the global healthcare market by assembling an arsenal of the most groundbreaking technology in existence.

It didn't matter who invented it. It didn't matter how I acquired it. What mattered was the outcome.

I'd assembled a world-class team here in Shenzhen. My company was poised to launch a broad range of technologies and services to providers all over the world. What my enemies didn't understand, what they failed to see in their panicked, emotional reactions, was that providing a unified approach to the market was the best thing for everyone. And I didn't just mean for the CEOs—I meant for every citizen of the world.

But Fiona and Lauren were too invested to see the big picture. Yet another reason I wished they were from any country other than America. As a rule, American women annoyed me. Fiona Pace's book about American women in the workplace *really* annoyed me. In it, she discussed at length how lots of women she knew withdrew from their careers because of guilt about their families and the competitive, demanding nature of corporate America. She suggested ways to remedy this so that women stayed in the workforce and achieved more senior and management positions.

Fiona's book pinpointed exactly what annoyed me most about American women. There was too much guilt. Always with the guilt, and the overanalyzing. They would tweet, whine, and workshop about the "hows" and the "whys" of women in the workplace, the existence of the glass ceiling and what to do about it, the existence of their *guilt* and what to do about it, when they should just shut up and keep working. If there was a glass ceiling, why not shatter it and grab a shard as a weapon? And if someone was in your way—like your boss or your husband? Wield the shard, elbow them out of the picture, then step on them with your high heel.

Otherwise, what were high heels for?

Despite their brilliance and their access to heels, I'd watched both Lauren and Fiona hesitate. In the current healthcare market, hesitation translated into death. Lauren had come to her senses and stopped sitting on her technology, but only after I'd threatened her. *That* seemed to have woken her up. But since she'd launched the patch, what else had she accomplished?

Nothing. And Fiona Pace was busy following suit. She'd conducted clinical trial after clinical trial, money and influence slipping through her fingers as she chased her tail. I'd offered her the opportunity to position her technology globally, to launch it as aggressively as possible.

And she'd turned me down.

I looked out the window at the bustling streets of Shenzhen. It was less foggy here than in Beijing, a fact I relished. They called my city the Silicon Valley of China, but soon, the titles would be reversed. That was on my short list of goals. I'd promised the people who worked for me and my government that Jiàn Innovations would deliver. We would put Shenzhen on the map, *in the center of technological and global influence.* In return, they'd promised their loyalty and unwavering support.

They were believers. And maybe, if I wasn't imagining it, they were a little afraid of me.

I thought about my apartment again, the bare walls and the bed I rarely slept in. I loved my home. I'd traded my boring, traditional life for the promise of my own mind. It was the same promise I'd made to my people, the same promise they saw in me.

Seeing was believing.

I'd failed to deliver Paragon and the patch, but I understood the power of failure. Now that I knew what didn't work, I would utilize what remained.

Because I knew the hard truth. Time wouldn't wait, and neither would I.

Chapter 5

HANNAH

Lauren hung up her cell phone and grabbed her laptop, shoving it into her bag. Gabe watched her, a deep *v* between his brows. "Babe?"

Lauren sighed. "That was Dave again. He said Li Na's team tried to hack us multiple times tonight. I'm going in."

I jumped up. "I'm coming with you."

Then I leaned down and kissed Wes good-bye quickly, before he could object.

"Want me to come, too?" Gabe asked.

"No, thanks. I can handle it." Lauren turned to me. "You don't need to go back to the office tonight—I can handle this. I just wanted you to know what was going on."

"I understand." I grabbed my tote anyway. "But I'm still coming."

We were quiet on the car ride to the lab. "Did you talk to Fiona again?"

I motioned with my phone. "She texted me a few minutes ago. She called the FBI and was wrapping some stuff up at the office. She's going to call Levi."

"Anything else?"

I shrugged. "She said she hadn't heard anything else from Li Na."

"That's because Li Na's busy hacking *us*." Lauren closed her eyes and shook her head. "She is an ever-loving pain in my ass."

I would've laughed—my sister rarely swore—but my nerves were too shot.

Our security guards, Timmy and Brian, hustled us into Paragon's lobby.

"What do you think she was trying to do?"

She sighed. "I don't know yet. But it's probably business as usual—she's trying to steal my technology."

I followed her down the hall to Dave and Leo's office. "You think she'd find a better way to spend her time."

"Well, she has, remember? She's hacking Fiona Pace now, too."

I shook my head. "With all the time she spends hacking and threatening, she could probably make some headway with research and development."

"I don't know. I don't think that's her business model. Now that I know she's going after Fiona, it looks like Li Na is more interested in acquisition by force."

I shuddered as we reached the office. "It would be better if she could find a willing partner."

"Agreed." Lauren paused before going in. "Listen, I appreciate you coming in and all, but you should probably go home. It's late, and honestly, you look tired. I don't need you coming back and working crazy hours right away. You need to take it easy."

"I *need* to find out what this bitch is doing inside our system again!"

She sighed. "Fine. I knew you were going to say that—even the 'bitch' part—but I was just doing my big-sister due diligence."

I raised my hands. "Just stop. Between you and Wes, I'm feeling over-diligenced."

"What do you mean? Is Wes worried about you, too? Because—"

"Lauren," Leo called from inside the office, "We need to show you something."

Lauren gave me one last suspicious look as we headed in. Leo and Dave's office was its characteristic mess, with empty takeout containers and candy bar wrappers littering every available surface. Both of them lived here. Like, literally. Dave had proudly told me at a meeting earlier in the day that he hadn't been home for three weeks.

Silicon Valley was like that. We wore our nonstop-work dark circles like badges of honor. Well, I used high-end concealer to cover up mine.

I cleared some empty coconut-water containers from a portion of the couch and warily sat down next to Dave, who wore scuffed Vans sneakers and a hoodie that looked as if he'd owned it since ninth grade. I hoped there weren't M&M's stuffed into the cushions like the last time I'd visited the guys. They'd stained my favorite skirt.

Leo, who looked more like a scruffy undergrad than a high-powered tech executive, hunched over his desk, tapping rapidly on his keyboard. Dave bounced his laptop on his bony knees. He held out a bag of Twizzlers to me.

I wrinkled my nose, disgusted by the unnaturally red candy. "No, thanks. And you should probably eat some real food—did you have dinner?"

Dave held up the Twizzlers, looking guilty.

"Ugh, how many times do I have to tell you two to eat normal meals? And to get outside and go for a walk? You're both so pale and skinny—"

"There it is," Leo said.

He pointed to the screen, and Lauren leaned over to see the piece of code.

"She put something in our firewall. I don't understand what it is. It's not a code I've seen before. And why would she do that?" Lauren asked, her brow furrowed. "As far as I know, she still wants my technology. She shouldn't be trying to destroy my system."

Leo scratched his patchy beard. "I'm not certain it's a virus, but I also don't understand what it's doing in our firewall. I need to check it out further. Have you heard anything from her—has she been in touch over the last few weeks?"

"No, not recently." Lauren's phone buzzed. "It's Gabe—I'll just be a second."

"Do you want me to order takeout for you?" I whispered to Dave. "I can get Japanese delivered. I can order you something with protein *and* vegetables remember them?"

"But I like Twizzlers," Dave whined.

"No—please tell me that isn't true," Lauren said into the phone, her voice too loud. Her shoulders shook.

I jumped up. "What is it?"

"I don't…I can't believe this is happening. I'll call you back." Lauren hung up and put her face in her hands. "That was Gabe. He just heard—Jim Pace was shot tonight. He's dead."

"Who's Jim Pace?" Dave asked.

Lauren's throat worked as she swallowed. "Fiona Pace's husband. Fiona Pace, the Protocol Therapeutics CEO."

Dave's brow furrowed. "I don't know who she is…"

Lauren's face was a pale mask. "She's Li Na Zhao's latest target. And now her husband's dead."

Chapter 6

WES

Gripping the kitchen island, I pulled myself up and pushed the wheelchair away—I hadn't technically been cleared for long-term standing, but after hearing about Jim Pace, I no longer gave a shit. I grimaced for a moment, catching my breath.

Then Gabe came into the kitchen, and I straightened myself. I had no intention of letting my strain show.

"Are your brothers on their way back?" I asked.

"Yeah, they're on the red-eye," Gabe said. "Fiona had just contacted them and hired them for personal security—right before this happened."

He was quiet for a long minute. "I can't believe Jim's dead. He and Fiona were college sweethearts. Jim was a great guy, brilliant—and he had a big heart. He loved his wife and his girls."

"They shot him right outside his office?"

Gabe grimaced. "Yeah. From what I heard, Jim had a late board meeting, and the parking lot was dark. He didn't have security—he'd never needed it. The shooter was waiting outside in a car. They used a silencer. One of the board members found Jim on the ground."

I gripped the island. "Jesus."

Gabe poured himself a drink. "They're going back through the security tape to see if they can ID the shooter or find plate numbers, but I doubt it'll help."

"What did Agent Marks say?"

Gabe had called his FBI contact as soon as he'd heard the news.

"The usual—thanks for the lead, and they're working on it."

I grimaced. "I don't have much use for Agent Marks."

Gabe flopped down into an armchair. "Tell me about it."

"What did Lauren say?"

I'd tried to call Hannah, but she hadn't picked up. They were still at Paragon.

"Not much. They're probably coming home soon." Gabe shook his head. "What a mess."

"We've got to be able to go after Li Na—get her arrested," I said. "She's committed too many crimes at this point. She's a freaking terrorist."

"Agent Marks has assured us at every step that there's nothing we can do because of jurisdiction."

I scrubbed a hand across my face. "Murdering and kidnapping can't get you incarcerated in China? That doesn't make any sense."

"It's a connectivity problem." Gabe took a sip of bourbon. "We can't actually prove that these thugs she's hiring work for her. There's no paper trail, no money trail, and there's no testimony. It's all circumstantial evidence, and that's not good enough. Maybe now that she's branched off and targeted another California company…*maybe* there's something we can do. I'm going to call Kami." He hopped up and headed for his office to call his lawyer. "I'll be back in a minute."

"Of course."

I waited until he left the room, and then I called Hannah again.

"Hey—sorry I didn't pick up before." She sniffled.

"Are you coming home?"

I knew they'd taken security with them to Paragon, but I couldn't help feeling panicked.

"We're on our way. We're fine. I'll see you soon."

But I could tell she was crying.

I hung up, and my mind raced, thoughts jumbling inside me. I knew Li Na was responsible for killing Jim Pace, but what was she thinking? What did she hope to accomplish with another round of violence? Apparently, losing Paragon hadn't dampened her enthusiasm for thug-like tactics. Li Na wanted Fiona Pace's company, but Fiona had said no.

And now Fiona's husband was dead.

I breathed a huge sigh of relief twenty minutes later when I heard Lauren and Hannah talking in the entryway. Brian came around the corner first.

"Any signs of trouble?" I asked him.

"Nothing."

"We need to make sure we have every available man on duty tonight," I instructed. "All eyes need to be on the perimeter, to make sure Li Na doesn't try something here, too."

Brian nodded. "I'll call everyone who's off-duty and have them come in."

"Thanks, buddy. Have you talked to Levi and Ash?"

"They'll be here in the morning."

He made himself scarce as Hannah rounded the corner, her eyes red and puffy from crying.

I held my arms out to her. "Hey."

She came toward me, then stopped. "Why are you out of the chair?"

I pulled her to my chest. "Don't we have bigger things to worry about?"

Lauren came in, looking exhausted as she unwrapped her scarf. "Where's Gabe?"

"He's in the office, on the phone with his lawyer."

"Okay." Lauren's gaze briefly met mine, then she looked pointedly at Hannah. "Hannah, you should get some rest—this has been a terrible shock. Have you heard from Fiona again?"

"No." Hannah's voice came out muffled against my chest. "Just that last text."

"What did she say?" I asked.

"She wanted to tell us about Jim." Hannah shook her head against me. "I can't believe this is happening again. I can't believe Li Na *killed Fiona's husband*."

I wrapped my arms around her. "It's going to be okay."

"Nothing's okay!" Hannah started crying. "They were married for fifteen years! They have two little girls!"

Lauren's face twisted with worry as she watched her sister. "Can I help?"

Hannah abruptly stopped crying and pulled back from me. She wiped her face roughly as she turned to her sister. "You just need to stay safe. We should *all* get some sleep, not just me—tomorrow's going to be a long day."

"Levi and Ash will be here first thing in the morning," I told them. "We'll get everyone together and have a debrief."

"That's good," Lauren said. "We're going to need to send a team to Protocol, and another team to watch Fiona and her girls."

Hannah shivered. "The poor things."

Lauren hugged her briefly, giving me another worried look as they embraced. She didn't have to say anything—I understood. She was concerned about Hannah, that this was too much for her little sister to bear.

Hannah pulled back from the embrace, but she still gripped Lauren's shoulders. "We're going to make her go away this time. She can't keep doing this."

Lauren blinked. She looked as though there were a million things she wanted to say, but she bit back the words.

Hannah turned to me. "I'm going to take a quick shower and go to bed. Are you coming?" Her gaze flicked briefly to the abandoned wheelchair.

"In a minute."

She opened her mouth and then closed it—probably about the chair—and then headed to our room.

Lauren started talking as soon as Hannah was out of earshot. "This is too much for her. Fiona is her friend, and we *just* saw her and talked to her. I don't know what this is going to do to her. We just got her back from those animals, and she's still so raw. I know she's trying to hold it all together—"

"She *is* holding it all together. She's tough. Maybe she's *too* tough."

Lauren went instantly on alert. "What do you mean?"

"I mean, I think she's dealing with all of this too well. I think she's holding stuff inside, and I don't know what to do to help her."

"Has she said anything?"

I shook my head, wondering if Hannah would make a shish kebab out of me for telling her sister about the nightmares. But here I was, about to talk, so I might as well prepare to be skewered. "She's been having nightmares. Bad ones. But she doesn't remember them, or she says she doesn't, and she doesn't want to talk about it."

Lauren started pacing. "I'll talk to her. I'll make her understand she doesn't have to hide this. Stress is nothing to be ashamed of—"

"Lauren." I waited until she stopped pacing. "We might need to give her some space—she *is* an adult. The most important thing right now is to protect her."

"Agreed." She started pacing again. I left her to it.

As I headed to my room, I had to stop frequently. I leaned against the wall, desperate to catch my breath and not pass out. I wiped my brow and composed my features as I reached the door.

It's my issue, and I'm dealing with it.

Hannah was in the shower. She came out a few minutes later in one of my T-shirts, her face puffy from crying.

"C'mere." I pulled down the comforter.

She shuffled into bed, clutching a tissue.

"I'm so sorry about your friend."

She blew her nose.

"It's okay, you know. It's okay to be scared."

She sat up a little, glaring. "I'm not scared."

"I meant sad," I backpedaled.

"I'm not sad—I mean, I'm sad, but that's not why I'm crying."

"Okay…" I waited to let her finish.

"I'm mad. And I'm not just mad, I'm so angry, I don't even know what to do. I've never felt this way before. It's like I'm out of control. If Li Na was in front of me right now, I don't even know what I'd do." She shook her head. "I hate hating her. But I hate her *so much*."

I held her closer. "I know how that feels."

Many times, in the service and on the job, I'd felt a blinding rage, an urge to crush someone.

"Do you feel like that now?"

I shook my head. "Right now, it's more like a dull throb. Like I'm the Hulk, and I'm getting ready to burst, but I'm not quite there yet. I'm more in the planning stage. I like to plan, *then* I like to burst. It's more effective that way."

A brief smile crossed Hannah's face. "I like that."

"Good." I wrapped my arms around her. "The Hulk's got you, babe, and there's extra security on the premises."

"What about Fiona?"

"Levi and Ash sent a team there. too. And the police are there. Her family's safe."

Now.

She looked as if she might start crying again, but I rocked her a little, holding her close.

"Go to sleep, babe. And tomorrow?"

She looked up at me expectantly.

"Tomorrow we plot our revenge."

She snuggled against my chest. "Plan, then burst."

I kissed the top of her head. "You got it."

Chapter 7

HANNAH

The burly guard leaned over my bed. "Hello, gorgeous."

"Fuck off."

He grabbed my arms and held them over my head. "You know, I never minded a little back talk. Sort of keeps things interesting."

"No! No! *No!*" I sat up suddenly, still thrashing, to find Wesley watching me, his bedside lamp turned on.

I scrubbed my hands over my face, wiping sleep from my eyes. "Oh. Sorry."

Wes gave me a long look. "You don't need to be sorry."

His voice sounded thick with emotion.

"Don't be upset—it was just a dream."

I scooted over toward him and rested my face against his chest.

"You're comforting *me*?"

I closed my eyes and didn't move.

"I want you to tell me what happened to you."

"Nothing happened to me."

"I want you to tell me." Emotion rolled off him in waves, but knowing I'd been through enough for one day, he kept his voice even.

I kissed his chest. "I already told you everything."

Still stricken about Jim Pace, it took every ounce of energy I had left to keep from bursting into another round of tears.

Wes pulled back and got out of bed.

Seeing him standing made me panic. "Babe, what are you doing?"

He didn't look at me. "I'm going to get some water."

I hopped out of bed. "I want some, too."

"I don't need a babysitter."

"I know you don't." The tears were close. "I just want to be with you."

His shoulder sagged. "Honey…"

I threw my arms around him and hugged him hard, harder than I'd dared to in the weeks since he'd come home from the hospital.

"I'm sorry I keep waking you up," I finally said.

"You're not. I was awake."

I pulled back and looked at him. "You're not sleeping?"

"Not tonight."

He shrugged, making the cords in his neck stand out, and I noticed that although he looked exhausted, he also looked more like himself. More muscular, more filled out—*stronger*.

"You look good, babe."

He started to laugh, surprising me. "I was just thinking the same thing about you."

"No, I mean it. You look more like your old self. Are you really feeling better?" I stroked his cheek. "Good enough to be out of your wheelchair?"

"It's time. I'll be fine."

"Can I come to your next doctor's appointment so I can ask Dr. Kim some questions?"

He gave me a tired smile, sinking back down on the bed. "Of course. I have an appointment later this week."

"Thanks, I'll be there. I don't know when Jim's service is going to be." I shook my head, the reality of the previous day catching up to me. "I can't believe this is happening. I can't believe someone shot Jim."

"I know."

His voice was soothing, and I let him pull me back under the covers and pull me against his massive chest.

"Try to go back to sleep—we still have a few hours."

I relished the feel of his arms around me, which I was getting used to. Before, he'd only slept over on the occasional night he was off-duty. Otherwise, he was awake guarding me or on the couch. I nestled against him, loving his warmth. *I'm getting spoiled.*

Safe in his embrace, I fell into a blissfully dreamless sleep, at least until my alarm went off.

I hopped out of bed, kissing Wes lightly as he slept. My follow-up appointment with Dr. Lourdes Fisher was first thing—a fact I'd kept to myself and my three security guards. Dr. Fisher had been hounding me to come back in. If I cancelled again, she'd be all over me. I had enough stress to deal with at the moment.

"We'll be back in time to meet with Levi and Ash to talk about increasing security. Please don't mention this appointment to anyone," I instructed Brian when we got to the office.

He frowned.

Brian was the lead guard assigned to me. He liked rules—following them, explaining them to others…following them.

"Okay?" I pleaded. "I don't feel like having Wes and Lauren ask me if I'm okay three million times today."

Brian didn't say anything. He just continued to frown, looking sour.

I ignored him as the nurse ushered me in. I changed into a faded, pastel-pink johnny. I didn't look at my body as I changed—I was pretty sure the bruises had faded, but I didn't want to see any trace.

The nurse weighed me. "You've gained back ten pounds," she said, checking my chart.

"Yay?" I said, trying lamely to make a joke.

"That's really good." She finished running through routine questions, updating my chart.

My knee bounced nervously as I waited for the doctor.

Dr. Fisher, who'd treated me and Lauren for years, smiled pleasantly when she came in. "It's nice to see you finally made it in here."

"I know. Sorry about that."

Her smile quickly turned to a frown when she saw me fidgeting. "How're you doing, Hannah?"

"I've been better." I wouldn't tell her about the nightmares, but I couldn't keep *everything* a secret. "A friend of mine was shot last night. He died."

The words tasted funny, sour, on my tongue.

"Oh my God, I'm so sorry." Dr. Fisher put a hand over her heart. "What happened?"

"We think it was more corporate espionage."

She peered at me over her glasses. "The same people?"

I sighed shakily and nodded.

"I'm so sorry. Are you having anxiety?"

"No. I'm…fine."

Dr. Fisher arched an eyebrow. "You'd have to be a superhero to be fine with all this. Do you want to talk about it?"

"No," I moaned. "I have to get back home for a meeting. Can we just get this over with?"

She laughed. "Gee, Hannah, tell me how you *really* feel."

"It's nothing personal. It's just that I know you're going to poke and prod me, and I don't feel like dealing with it—which is why I've cancelled my last three appointments."

"Fair enough. I'm just glad you finally came in." She smiled, warmth and concern lighting up her face. "But now it's time to poke and prod. You ready?"

I sighed and tried to relax on the exam table, but the paper underneath me crinkled. *Ugh.*

"Sure."

Dr. Fisher checked my chart. "Your weight gain's good. That's solid progress. Are you exercising yet?"

Before I'd been kidnapped, I was an avid runner, hot-yoga devotee, and I'd joined a barre gym. But I hadn't even glanced at my sneakers since I'd been home. "Not really—I've been walking a little, pushing Wesley around the grounds. I'm just trying to make sure he's getting enough fresh air."

"You don't need to exercise until you feel up to it, but don't forget to make time for yourself, okay?"

"I'll get back to it when I can."

I was about to say *when things get back to normal*, but that seemed too optimistic.

"Fine." Dr. Fisher smiled. "How is Wesley doing? He's been home for a couple of weeks now, correct? What's the prognosis?"

I swallowed. "The best news is there's no brain damage, even though he had head trauma. Dr. Kim from El Camino says that he'll make a full recovery, but he needs to go slow. Because he was in a coma and in bed for so long, his muscles are weak. I know he wants to quit using his wheelchair, and he's really pushing himself. I think he's having a hard time."

"Does he seem depressed?" Dr. Fisher asked.

"No..." Was Wesley depressed, or just frustrated? "Maybe."

"Let me know if you want a referral for a therapist. For *either* of you—you've both been through a lot, especially with what's just happened."

"Um, thanks, but I don't think that'll be necessary."

"Have you two had intercourse yet?"

Dr. Fisher sounded clinically casual, but I could hear her concern.

I picked at the johnny. "No. Wes isn't cleared yet."

"Is your sex drive normal?"

"I don't know. I think so? I'm not really thinking about it. There's too much going on."

Dr. Fisher wrote something in her notes. "Lie back and we'll start the exam. My hands are pretty cold—sorry."

She was silent as she worked, pressing on my ribs, palpating my stomach. She listened to me breathe, her stethoscope, which was even colder than her hands, pressed against me. I *hated* going to the doctor. I'd never liked it, but I didn't want any extra scrutiny after being kidnapped. All these questions and everyone fussing over me was starting to drive me nuts—we had a *murderer* on the loose. Who the hell needed a palpated abdomen?

"I think we should do a full gynecological exam and a pap today, okay?"

I sat up a little. "Why?"

Dr. Fisher arranged the stethoscope around her neck. "Because I want to make sure everything's okay. I examined you when you got home, but I need to be thorough."

"Fine. But I really do need to get going." My voice sounded tiny.

"It'll just take a minute."

She started the examination, and I forced myself to think about something else, something pleasant, anything but Jim Pace and poor Fiona and the girls. I racked my brain until I thought of the perfect distraction: Lauren's wedding. She wanted to hold off picking a date, but I hoped she'd change her mind. In the interim, I continued to dress-shop for her—even though she'd made me cancel all the appointments I'd made with bridal salons.

Not that I was going to let a little thing like *that* stop me.

Still, as Dr. Fisher examined me, I pictured the strapless lace gown I'd picked out for Lauren. My sister would *kill it* in that dress. I just had to convince her to try it on…

"I'm just going to insert the speculum," Dr. Fisher said.

"Oh, joy." I winced as I felt the cold metal inside me, but she was mercifully quick.

Her back was to me as she cleaned up. "Hannah, is there anything you want to tell me?"

"N-no." My chest squeezed. "Is everything okay?"

"Everything looks fine." Her voice was soothing. "But we never went into detail about what happened while you were held captive. There was never any evidence of trauma, but I've been practicing medicine for three decades, and I can tell when something is off. Hannah, were you sexually assaulted?"

"No one raped me." I wanted to scrunch my eyes shut, but I forced myself to relax my face.

"There are other types of sexual assault."

"I told you—I'm fine."

"Are you having any difficulty—trouble sleeping, anxiety, anything like that?"

"Wes said I've had a couple of nightmares, but I don't remember them."

Dr. Fisher came back to the table and patted my arm. "If there's anything you want to tell me, now is the perfect time. Sometimes it's easier to talk to a person you have a professional relationship with than it is to talk to your family."

Jesus, is this some sort of conspiracy?

"I'm fine, really." I sat up and grabbed my clothes.

"Are you having any symptoms of depression or panic? Any heart racing? Jumpiness?"

"No, no, and no," I said, trying to keep from sounding snippy and failing. "But I appreciate you being thorough."

Dr. Fisher pursed her lips and handed me several handouts. I glanced at them briefly: *Anxiety, Depression, and PTSD – Symptoms and Treatment.*

"Gee, thanks, but I don't need these. What happened to me wasn't that traumatic."

"You were kidnapped, beaten, and drugged by strangers. They didn't feed you, and you were dehydrated. They almost shot you." Dr. Fisher held her clipboard against her chest. "Don't minimize what you went through. It was most certainly traumatic. And now there's what happened to your friend. If it were me, I'd take something or talk to someone. There's no shame in it."

"I really do feel fine." But even as the words came out of my mouth, I felt like I might cry. I needed to get out of here.

"Sometimes the symptoms sneak up on you," she said gently. "I just want you to be aware that having some anxiety or other issues after all this is perfectly normal. So read the sheet and know the signs. If you ever want to talk, just text me."

"Thank you, I appreciate it. But I really need to get to work now."

Dr. Fisher arched an eyebrow, but at least she let me go.

I called Fiona from the car on the ride home.

"Hannah." She was clearly sobbing.

"I'm so sorry."

Fiona blew her nose but kept crying. "You told me. You warned me, but I didn't move fast enough."

I shook my head, tears streaming down my own face. There was so much *pain* in her voice. "This wasn't your fault. There's nothing you could've done."

"She wanted my company." Her voice shook. "And Jim paid for that."

I felt helpless. "Can I come over? Can I help with the girls?"

"My mom's here. I'll—I'll talk to you later."

I went to say "okay," but she'd already hung up. And really, what was the point of using that stupid word today?

My friend's world had fallen apart. There was no such thing as "okay."

I wrapped my arms around myself, forcing back the tears. Instead, I pictured Li Na Zhao's face. I pictured punching it, hard, again and again.

Because angry felt better than sad. Hell yes, it did.

So I kept the image in my mind all the way home.

Chapter 8

WES

I cursed myself for keeping my early morning appointment as I glared at Ashley, my physical therapist. "You're not seriously making me do this."

She crossed her arms. "Come on, tough guy. You can *totally* do this."

"I know—because I've already done it three times."

"So do it again. No big deal, right?"

I blew out a deep breath and looked at the mat. She wanted me to hold the plank position for as long as I could. Sweat ran in rivulets down my chest, and my arms and legs were already shaking. Over the past couple of weeks, Ashley had been coming to the house, running me through various exercises down in Gabe's massive home gym. Our goal was to get me stronger, strong enough to tolerate walking on my own and to increase my muscle mass.

My ultimate goal, of course, was to kick Li Na Zhao's ass.

"Get going," Ashley grunted.

I might have to kick Ashley's ass, too.

I mentally referred to her as Evil Spawn. Even though she was young, dark-skinned, dreadlocked, and perpetually dressed in blue scrubs and running shoes, Ashley reminded me of Sergeant Dell, my drill sergeant from basic training. Sgt. Dell was pasty-white and paunchy, with graying hair, in his mid-fifties—but like Ashley, he'd been crusty and ruthless. He'd also been utterly convinced and openly vocal about his prediction we would all fail.

Sergeant Dell motivated me. I felt the same way about Ashley—she pissed me off, so I wanted to prove something to her.

"I'm waiting," she said, her muscular arms folded against her chest. "And last time I checked, I wasn't getting any younger. You aren't, either."

"Sadist," I said under my breath.

Ashley tilted her chin, her dreads swishing. "I heard that."

I *thought* I'd said it under my breath.

I struggled to hold form, silently cursing her—but this time I made sure I actually kept silent. I made it for another full minute and collapsed against the mat, my arms shaking, my legs jelly. My heart thudded in my chest, a fact I kept to myself.

"Wes?" Ashley actually sounded a little worried. "Are you okay?"

"Oh, I'm great. I can barely do a plank without feeling like I'm going to die, but really, I've never been better."

"Good."

Now she sounded like her smug, punishing self.

"I'm pretty sure I don't like you," I said.

"I get that a lot." She came over and smiled down at me, offering her hand. "How about we make a deal? One year from now, you're running a half marathon with me—and by the way, I *hate* running. It's *sooo* boring. But I'll do it for you so we both have something to work toward."

"Half marathons are for weenies," I croaked, knowing this would piss her off. "If you want to talk about running a full, I'm in. Because I'm no weenie."

"Fine. But sit up. It's time for leg raises."

"Are you trying to kill me?"

She shrugged. "If you ever call me a weenie again, I just might."

Chapter 9

HANNAH

"Isn't there any legal way to proceed against her?" I asked Levi soon after the meeting started.

Levi sighed and rubbed his eyes, which were bloodshot from his overnight flight, as we all waited for an answer. Ten of Betts Security's top agents crowded the living room, along with myself, Wes, Ash, Gabe, and Lauren. Timmy, Lauren's longtime personal security guard, and Gabe's and Lauren's attorneys, Kami Robards and Bethany O'Donnell, were also present.

"Yeah, there's a legal way," Levi said. His carefully pressed pink button-down shirt strained against his powerful chest, a striking juxtaposition of expensive Italian style and unadulterated, Boston-homegrown-street-fighting brawn. "We could get her prosecuted here in California in federal court, and we can ask for her extradition. But do I think that the Chinese government's going to cooperate with that? No, I do not. Even if they did, Li Na would know far enough in advance that she could go into hiding. The other issue is that even if we managed to get her into an American court, the evidence against her is strictly tangential."

Kami, immaculate in a navy suit, raised her hand. "I would think there's enough circumstantial evidence at this point to get a conviction."

Bethany shook her head, shoulder-length blonde hair swaying. "I don't know." She frowned. "Reasonable doubt is a tough standard. We would need at least one strong connection, one solid piece of evidence tying Li Na to the men she's hired over here to commit the crimes. I'm guessing it's not going to be easy to locate corroborating evidence—she's shown over and over again that she covers her tracks. So even if we get her extradited and indicted, which sounds like a long shot, we might not be able to make charges stick."

Levi watched Bethany with interest, finally tearing his gaze away to address the rest of us. "Right. Attorney O'Donnell is correct, and I don't think we can look for an extradition and a court proceeding as Plan A. I wish it were different, but that's not the world we're living in."

"What about a private strike against her?" Wesley asked. "Is your firm equipped to handle a mission like that?"

"We're equipped for all sorts of things, but Lauren and Gabe have made it clear in the past that they don't want to physically harm Li Na. They don't want blood on their hands, and I support that."

"What other options do we have?" I asked, near outrage. *Li Na can't get away with murdering my friend's husband! After everything she's done—killing Clive Warren, terrorizing my sister, what she did to me, Wesley, and now Jim Pace—she needs to pay.* My blood boiled at the injustice. Now *I* felt like the Hulk, about to burst.

"Not many." Levi shrugged. "Right now, our focus needs to stay on security. Security at home, security at Paragon and Dynamica, and security for Fiona Pace and her family."

I clenched my hands into fists, frustration rolling through me. "I don't…I don't want to just focus on defense. We need to go after her. She can't just keep getting away with what she's doing. She's a *criminal*. She's a corporate *terrorist*. We need justice, not babysitting!"

"Hannah," Lauren said in a low tone.

"No, she's right." Levi scrubbed a hand across his face. "But we still need to start with security. I'm imposing a curfew, and I need a daily agenda from each of you—Hannah, Lauren, Gabe, Wesley, Kami, and Bethany. I need to know where you are every second of every day, and who you're with. We'll be screening any unknowns, so you need to be prepared for that."

Bethany tapped her pink pen against her pink laptop case, nervous energy radiating off her. "Um, I'm sorry, but I have a busy practice to run. I meet new clients every day, and I don't have time to vet everything through a committee."

"Fine." Levi frowned. "I'll just assign one of my guys to you—so you can run everything by one man, not a committee. But your agent needs to come with you everywhere."

"This isn't going to work for me—" Bethany spluttered.

"Randy, you are hereby assigned to Bethany." Levi waved at one of the guards in the back, an enormous, grizzled-looking man in his mid-forties with tattooed knuckles. He was thickly muscled and built broadly, like a refrigerator, one of the Viking ones with double doors. He came over and sat by Bethany, grunting at her in greeting.

She grunted back. "You can't bring weapons into court," she instructed Randy.

"Yes, ma'am."

"And don't call me ma'am."

"Yes, Attorney O'Donnell." Randy offered her a small smile.

She smiled back. "You learn fast—that's at least in your favor."

"Appears you two will get along fine," Levi said, clearly pleased with himself.

Bethany glared at him. "I don't like being told what to do."

"Duly noted, Attorney O'Donnell. Any further objections?"

She scowled and tapped her pen.

"Timmy, you're with Lauren. Ash, stick with Gabe."

Timmy nodded. Ash and Gabe both groaned.

"Brian, you're still with Hannah—"

Wes raised his hand. "Actually, Levi, I'd like to watch Hannah. I'm a Paragon employee, though, so I guess I need permission from Lauren." He leaned forward and looked to her, silently begging. "I'm cleared for most physical activity. I can do this, and I want to be close by in case something happens."

I couldn't believe my ears. "Wes, *no*. You just got out of your wheelchair, which I'm not even remotely sure is authorized—"

He squeezed my hand. "Babe? This isn't your decision. Lauren?"

I stopped talking and furiously turned my attention to my sister.

Lauren's shoulders sagged. "I don't know if it's a good idea."

"Brian will be there, too. I'm not going to compromise Hannah's safety by trying to do this alone. But I need to be there to protect her. I can walk now. I don't need the wheelchair anymore—"

"Wes, we need to talk," Levi said. "After the meeting, okay? We'll figure it out then."

"Okay," Wes said. He didn't dare look in my direction.

Levi went on to discuss the security plans for Jim Pace's service, which was happening the next morning, but I couldn't focus on his words. Lauren and I were going to Fiona's house later today, and I felt sick for my grieving friend. That, plus what Wes had just pulled, combined to make me a hot mess.

When the meeting wrapped up, and I grabbed Wes's hand. "I need to talk to you."

"I have to talk to Levi first."

"I'm coming with you," I insisted.

Wes cursed under his breath, but he held on to my hand and headed toward Levi, who was addressing Randy and the guard assigned to Kami Robards.

"I want to know every detail. I want you to run a background check on everyone in their offices, and I want you to send me a copy of their schedules. You are to be in *every* meeting."

Bethany elbowed her way into the conversation. "Have you ever heard of the term 'attorney-client privilege'? I can't bring a meat locker into a client meeting! No offense, Randy."

"None taken, Attorney O'Donnell."

Levi's jaw clenched as he leaned over Bethany, apparently trying to menace her. "You can't be alone right now. It's not safe."

He obviously didn't know our lawyer very well—she stood up even straighter, all five foot three of her in spiked heels, and didn't back down an inch. "I've been taking care of myself for a long time, and quite successfully. *I don't need your help.*"

Levi crossed his arms. "Lauren agrees with me about this, and last time I checked, she was your boss."

Bethany arched an eyebrow. "Lauren is my *client*—I tell *her* what to do, not vice versa. So back *off.*"

Lauren came over and patted Bethany on the arm. "Can you please take security as a favor for your favorite client? I don't want you getting hurt. I can't handle worrying about it right now. So please, take Randy with you. If you're worried about privilege, just let him background check everyone and then he can wait outside the door of whatever meeting you have. Okay?"

Bethany frowned at Lauren. "Okay." She turned back to Levi. "For the record, I like being asked—not told."

Levi's eyes glittered. "Duly noted."

Bethany snorted. "Enough with the legalese. Jesus!" She stalked off, Randy close on her clicking heels.

Levi watched Bethany as she left, and Lauren watched Levi. I wondered if my sister had neglected to tell me some juicy gossip, and vowed to corner her about it later.

Wes stepped forward. "Levi."

All concerns about gossip fell away. I gripped Wes's hand so he wouldn't forget about me and what *I* wanted, which was to keep him as far from harm's way as possible.

"You said you wanted to talk to me," Wes said.

"I do." Levi's gaze flicked to me. "How're you doing, Hannah?"

"I'm good. Thanks." Since Levi and his team had rescued me, he'd continued to check in on me, the way a big brother might. "But I don't want Wes coming back to active duty—he hasn't been cleared for that."

Wes ignored me and focused on Levi. "I have a follow-up appointment with my doctor later this week."

"Good." Levi patted Wes's arm. "We'll see about getting you back in the field after that. But, I do need to talk to you—Lauren and I have been discussing Paragon's security, and she'd like my company to take over operations at the lab."

Eddie, Paragon's long-time security manager, had decided to retire. Who could blame him?

"Okay." But Wes sounded unsure.

Levi smiled at him. "I'd like you to come work for Betts Security. You'll still be at Paragon on a rotating basis, but business is booming in Silicon Valley. I need all the good men I can get, including you and your brother. I spoke to Ellis last night, by the way. He'll be here this afternoon."

Wes coughed. "*Here*, here? As in Northern California?"

"Yes, he said he'd stop by after he dropped his stuff at home. Listen, about your new position, I'll send you the contract so you can review it. I have your number. You can start as soon as you're medically cleared." Levi patted him on the arm again and was gone.

I temporarily stopped being pissed about Wes's campaign to get back to work. "Ellis will be here this afternoon. That's great!"

He grunted, looking less than ecstatic. "We, as in you and me, are going real estate shopping. I'll let my brother have my old house—him and his guns and his Budweiser."

I didn't think Wes really needed to add house hunting to his to-do list. Selfishly, the idea of him going anywhere, including to a new house of his own, made my gut twist. But I needed to be supportive, at least about this.

"We can start looking. I'll help," I offered.

"It's a date. Listen, can I come with you to Fiona's today? I promise I won't act like a security guard, just a worried boyfriend."

"Wes!" Brian called from the other side of the room. "We need you for a tactical meeting in five."

I bristled. "Already getting back to work, huh?"

"I can do tactics sitting in the comfort of Gabe and Lauren's living room," he chided, "so you don't have to worry. I guess I can't come with you, though."

"Levi and Ash are going with us—they want to talk to Fiona about coverage for the service and setting up personal security for the girls. Lauren and I will be fine."

Wes brushed the hair from my forehead, still looking at me with concern. "Are you okay about this? Seeing her?"

I squared my shoulders. "I have to be. She needs me."

"You don't have to be so strong for everybody all the time."

An image of Wes lying in his hospital bed, unconscious, with tubes running into his body, flashed in my mind. I threw my arms around his neck. "Yes, I do."

Chapter 10

HANNAH

Ash maneuvered up the Paces' long driveway. Their home was on the other side of Palo Alto in a gated community. Then the large stucco house came into view, replete with columns and a bubbling fountain adorning the manicured lawn.

Ash let out a low whistle as we got out of the SUV. "This is gorgeous."

Levi grunted, looking around at the sunshine and the rolling green lawn. "California really is nicer than Massachusetts—it's not fair."

"Right?" Ash agreed. "Palo Alto makes South Boston look like it got beat with the ugly stick. Which it sort of did, but still."

"How old are Fiona's kids again?" Levi asked me as we walked the path to the front door.

I winced. "Her daughters are eight and six—Katie and Quinn. They're the sweetest little girls. Fiona said they're absolutely crushed. Jim was a great dad."

Levi seemed at a loss for words—he'd lost his own dad when he was young. He just shook his head, composing his features as we ascended the walkway.

An older woman opened the front door, and even though I'd never met her, I immediately recognized her as Fiona's mother. "I'm Hannah Taylor, a friend of Fiona's. This is my sister, Lauren, and part of our security detail, Levi and Asher Betts. They run Betts Security."

The woman held out her hand. "I'm Evelyn Bartlett, Fiona's mom. She's expecting you."

She motioned for us to come in, and I saw Katie and Quinn sitting on a long bench in the foyer, their faces blotchy from crying. They waved to me, then resumed clutching their somewhat beat-up stuffed animals.

I bent down to see them, careful to give them space. "Hey, girls. I'm so sorry about your dad."

Usually, whenever I came to the house, they were all over me—asking me about my clothes and if I wanted to play dolls. Today, they barely looked up. "Thanks," they mumbled in unison.

Their grandmother gently kissed them both. "I'm going to bring Hannah and her friends to see your mom, and then we can go to the kitchen for a snack, okay?"

Katie nodded. Quinn just stroked her stuffed bunny's matted ears.

Mrs. Bartlett shook her head as she led us to the living room. "Those poor girls. They haven't stopped crying and asking for their dad. This is just—it's unbearable."

Fiona sat in the far corner of a room decorated in varying shades of white and cream. With the sun pouring through the windows, the large room should have been cheerful. But seeing Fiona wrapped in a blanket next to the fireplace, her face a pale, puffy mask, sucked any joy from the atmosphere.

I willed myself not to cry as I went to my friend and wrapped my arms around her. "I'm so sorry."

"Thank you." Fiona pulled back, and I could see dark circles, like bruises, underneath her eyes. She hugged Lauren and motioned for us all to sit.

"Mrs. Pace, I'm so sorry to hear about your husband," Levi said. "And I know this is painful for you, but I need you to tell me everything that happened when Jim was killed, and everything that's happened since."

Fiona wrapped the blanket back around her. "I've already made a statement to the police and to the FBI."

"I want you to know that we work with law enforcement, and we cooperate with them fully. But if you decide to finalize things with our firm, you'll want us to know everything. We might see something that the other agencies miss."

Fiona nodded, then closed her eyes for a moment and breathed deeply, calming herself. When she opened her eyes a moment later, she looked directly at Levi. "Jim stayed late at the office for a board meeting. He left around eight o'clock. The security tape shows him walking to his car and then staggering a little and collapsing before he could open the door. There was no audio, but the other board members said they didn't hear anything—the police think the gunman used a silencer. When they reached him, he was already dead. He was shot in the heart. The police said he died instantly."

I forced myself to stay calm. If Fiona could be brave enough to tell us the story, I needed to listen without giving in to my emotions.

"Any information about the assailant's vehicle?" Ash asked.

"They traced it to a rental place, but the car was rented under a fake name and just led to a dead end."

"Do you have any idea who's behind this?" Ash asked.

Fiona looked from me to Lauren. "It was Li Na Zhao. She...she threatened me a few weeks ago, saying that if I didn't sell my company's technology to her, she would make me sorry. I declined her offer. I went and spoke to Hannah and Lauren about it because it seemed like a direct threat. They agreed. But I never thought this would happen to Jim. I didn't take any steps to protect him." She winced and turned away, facing the fire instead.

"This isn't your fault." Lauren reached out and took Fiona's hand. "Li Na doesn't do what you'd expect, and *no one* could have prepared you for this. Have you...heard anything from her?"

"I got a letter from her lawyer. It was a proposal."

"Was it from Petra Hickman?" Lauren asked. "I thought Li Na would have fired her."

Petra had represented Li Na in her attempt to buy Paragon from Lauren. It hadn't ended well.

Fiona shook her head. "No—it was from a business attorney in Cupertino. Someone I've never heard of. I didn't respond."

"I need that letter," Levi said immediately. "Li Na hasn't reached out to you directly or claimed any sort responsibility for your husband's death?"

"No. She hasn't. I wouldn't expect her to—would you?"

"She was very straightforward when she kidnapped Hannah." Lauren's gaze flicked to me. "But that was different, I suppose."

"Because Hannah was still alive." Fiona's voice was flat.

"Did you tell the police and the FBI about Li Na's proposal and the timing of the correspondence from her attorney?" Ash asked, his voice gentle.

"Yes," Fiona said. "But they didn't think there was anything they could do. They need more evidence."

Levi leaned forward. "We'll come up with a plan to deal with Zhao—I promise you that. But we need to focus on your safety and your daughters' safety. If you're comfortable talking about what my company can do for you, I think we should."

"Please. Go on."

Fiona wrapped herself deeper into her blanket as Levi and Ash outlined the personal security services they could offer, along with what a Betts Security team could do at Protocol. I watched as Fiona listened carefully, asking pertinent questions and assimilating the information. Even in her grief, she was alert and astute.

"When the girls go back to school, how would that work with personal security agents?"

"That's the most important thing." Ash nodded. "We can talk to the school administration—we've handled situations like this before. Our goal is to keep the child safe at all times, while minimizing the impact of having a security detail with them."

They kept talking while my mind wandered to Katie and Quinn. Their two little faces, puffy from crying, and the way they clung to their stuffed animals. I dug my fingernails into my palms to stop the tears. Those poor little things, having their father taken from them like this…

I hugged Fiona fiercely before we left, promising to see her at the service tomorrow. On the ride home, as Levi and Ash discussed the logistics of their new security assignment, Lauren looked at me with concern. "You're awfully quiet."

I looked out the window, away from her. "It was the girls."

She reached over and took my hand in hers. "I know. It's terrible to see them suffer like that. They're innocent."

"I just don't understand. I mean, I don't understand any of what she's done."

"Who?"

"Li Na." I pulled my hand away. "I don't understand how she could have Jim killed just because she wants in on Protocol Therapeutics's profit margin."

"But that's not all she wants," Lauren said. "She wants what comes *with* that—the notoriety, the importance. Gabe has a whole theory about her."

"I'll have to ask him." I watched cars fly by on the freeway, feeling unsettled and angry.

My thoughts eventually circled back to Fiona. Seeing my friend's quiet devastation had gutted me. "I don't even know what to say about what Fiona's going through…"

Lauren sighed. "I don't, either—but you and I both know you can't get over losing someone suddenly." Lauren and I had direct experience with this. Our parents had died in a car crash. "All we can do is be here for their family."

"And get rid of Li Na," I said bitterly.

Lauren patted my hand. "Yeah. That would help."

* * *

I let the hot water rush over me as I combed my hair and put more conditioner in. I didn't ever want to get out of the shower. I wanted to stay under the warm water, pretend everything was normal, and forget my friend's husband had been murdered by the woman who'd been chasing my sister for the past year.

Lauren and Fiona were both trying to make the world a better place with their technology. They wanted to *help* people, but they were being targeted and punished for their visionary technological advances.

I closed my eyes as I rinsed my hair, but I kept seeing the Pace girls in my mind. I remembered when my parents had died—I'd been sixteen. When the police had come to the house and said there'd been an accident, I didn't believe them. No one drove more slowly or safely than my father in his Subaru station wagon. I'd made the officer take me to the morgue at the hospital before I believed they were dead.

But then I saw them. They *were* dead.

I shivered as I turned the water off, then wrapped myself in a towel. I didn't want to think about my parents. I didn't want to think about the poor Pace girls. But I *couldn't* stop the flood of thoughts about Fiona and her girls and what they were going through right now—what Li Na Zhao had done to them, done to all of us. I started to blow dry my hair as my thoughts zigzagged around, making me feel dizzy. I pictured Jim Pace dead, his body sprawled in the parking lot. Wesley, hooked up to all those tubes. Those little girls' faces, the way they'd clung to their favorite stuffed animals. I'd dug out my old teddy bear and slept with it after my parents died. It had smelled familiar, a scent memory from my childhood. I'd wept against it, begging to go back in time.

I kept working on my hair, but suddenly I realized that I was having a hard time catching my breath. I put the blow dryer down and threw on my favorite Stanford T-shirt and a pair of sweats. Every time I exhaled, I felt my body shake. I held up my hands—they were shaking, too.

What the hell?

Feeling dizzy, I sank down onto the terracotta floor. I leaned my back against the wall and did yoga breathing—in through the nose, out through the mouth. I tried to clear my mind and concentrate on my breathing, but it was as though the floodgates had opened. The images wouldn't stop coming.

Those poor girls. Their little faces. I felt a hole in my chest as I ached for them.

Wesley in the hospital bed, pale as death.

Jim Pace sprawled in the parking lot.

Wesley getting shot in front of me in the kitchen. He went down and slammed his head on the marble island. I'd thought he was dead.

I'd thought I'd never see him again.

The morgue at the hospital when I was sixteen. I could never forget what my mother's face had looked like, waxen but calm. *Dead.*

Dead, dead, dead.

I tried to catch my breath, and I heard myself gasp. I gulped for air as my whole body shook. My hands curled into fists, and I felt tears stream down my face. *Breathe, Hannah.* But I couldn't. I was hyperventilating.

And the images kept coming.

Gabe shooting the driver in Oakland, the window splintering into a million tiny cracks.

The burly guard standing over me in the dark. I could feel his breath on my face.

The hollowed-out, flat look in Fiona Pace's normally vibrant eyes.

"Wes," I croaked desperately. "Wes." But my voice didn't raise above a whisper. My heart hammered in my chest, and the tears poured freely now. I could hear my ragged, wheezing breaths. *Am I having a heart attack?* I tried to raise my hand to bang on the door, but I couldn't get my arms to cooperate.

"Wesley." I tried to yoga breathe, but I wondered if this was it, if all the stress was finally getting to me and I was going to die like this, on my sister's stylishly tiled bathroom floor in my ratty Stanford T-shirt.

"Help," I said as my body shook. "Help!"

I heard Wesley in the bedroom. "Babe? You in there?"

I struggled to get enough air to breathe and to call for him. "Wes. Wesley!" I tried to scream, but it came out like a hoarse whisper.

He knocked on the door. "Hannah? Did you call me?"

I started sobbing. "Wes…Wes, open the door."

He opened the door and stuck his head in. When he saw me on the floor, he rushed in and immediately put his hands on my face. "Hannah? Talk to me."

"I can't—I can't breathe," I wheezed. "And my hands are numb. They curled into fists, and they're numb. I can't move them."

"Okay." Wes leaned down and grabbed my wrist, checking my pulse. He counted silently for a moment, his brow knitted in concentration. When he'd finished, he asked calmly, "What are you feeling?"

"I think I might be having a heart attack." I struggled for a breath.

"I'm going to get you the help you need. Hold on. I'm right here—I've got you." He stood up for one second, never letting go of me, and leaned out the door. *"Lauren!"*

I thought I heard movement from the hall, but I couldn't be sure. I kept trying to catch my breath.

"Breathe, baby. I'm going to call an ambulance."

"No—no!"

But he was already in the bedroom, on the phone. He came back immediately as he called 9-1-1. "I have a twenty-five-year-old female with signs of tachycardia. She's having trouble breathing." He gave them our address and put the phone down. "They'll be here in a few minutes. Stay with me, babe." He sat down next to me on the floor, gripping my clawlike hand. "Let's breathe together."

"Wes? Wes!" Lauren came around the corner, and her eyes went wild when she saw me. *"Hannah!"*

"She's okay. Her pulse is high, but she's okay—the paramedics are on their way. I think she's having a panic attack."

I shut my eyes, sobbing and trying to breathe. I didn't want them to see me like this. It was so fucking mortifying.

"What can I do?" Lauren sounded panicked.

"Go wait at the door for the ambulance—bring the paramedics in here and tell them she needs oxygen. They'll have everything we need."

I heard Lauren run for the door, and Wes leaned against me, stroking my hair. "Shh, it's okay. We're going to get you the help you need, and you're going to be okay."

"I don't—I don't know what's happening." I squinted my eyes open and looked at my hands, which were still curled like claws. "Why are my hands like that?"

"It happens. I've seen it happen to my buddies. Shh, now, they're almost here."

Wesley kept talking to me gently and breathing with me, and as the minutes passed, I started to feel myself able to take a full breath.

"That's my girl. Good girl," he said.

My shoulders shook with sobs. "I'm so sorry."

"You have nothing to apologize for. I'm sorry you're going through this—but you are going to be okay, and I'm not leaving your side."

"O-okay. Okay."

The paramedics came in then, and I cringed away, embarrassed that my breathing was returning to normal and I was not, in fact, on the verge of death. The first one through the door, a young Asian woman, immediately wrapped a blood pressure cuff around my bicep and put an oxygen mask over my face.

The influx of oxygen helped me catch my breath. I managed to breathe a sigh of relief.

The paramedic was everywhere at once. "What's her name?" she asked Wes.

"Hannah."

"Hannah, I'm Kerry, and I'm here to help." She checked my blood pressure. "Good. It's within normal range. Are you on any medication?"

"No." I tried to move my hands, but they still wouldn't unclench.

"Nothing? Vitamins, supplements, anything?" She hooked up some electrodes to my chest and checked their connection to a machine. "This is an EKG, by the way—to check your heart rate. Now, about the medications?"

"I was on birth control, but I haven't taken them in a while…" With everything going on, I'd completely forgotten to take my pills.

"Have you ever had any trouble with your heart before, or is there any family history of heart attack?"

"No."

Kerry read the EKG results, smiling at me reassuringly. "Everything looks fine."

"Is she okay?" Lauren asked. I hadn't realized she'd been watching, and I didn't have to look at her to tell she was crying.

"She is—she's going to be just fine. Do you mind waiting outside? I want to give her some air." She looked from Lauren to Wes.

"Okay," Lauren said, but she didn't sound okay.

"Babe?" Wes hadn't budged from my side.

"I'm fine," I croaked, "but please take care of Lauren."

Wes squeezed my hand one last time and left me alone with Kerry. The two other paramedics came into the bathroom, entering notes into their tablets and picking up the equipment Kerry had used.

"Are you feeling better?" She had a calm, efficient tone that I appreciated.

"Yes, I can breathe better now." Still, my shoulders shook with sobs. "I'm just embarrassed—was that…did I just have a panic attack?"

Kerry slowly massaged my hands, working my fingers open and helping me flex them. "Are you having numbness in your fingers still?"

"It's like they fell asleep—they're tingling, but the feeling's coming back."

"Have you ever had a panic attack before?" Kerry asked.

"No. Never. I thought I was having a heart attack."

She watched me carefully. "Any history of anxiety or depression?"

"No."

"Any recent trauma? Boyfriend trouble?"

"No boyfriend trouble, but there's been a lot going on. A friend of mine lost her husband this week—he was murdered."

"I'm so sorry." She checked my blood pressure again and motioned for the paramedics to give me some tissues.

I took the oxygen mask off and unceremoniously blew my nose—I'd already humiliated myself in front of these people. It didn't matter if I blew my nose too loud.

"Your blood pressure's back to normal now, and so is your heart rate."

"Great." I forced myself to smile at her. "So we made you come out here for nothing."

Kerry cocked her head. "Not so fast. How long did this episode last?"

"I don't know. A few minutes? Maybe a little longer?"

"I'm going to watch you for another ten minutes to make sure nothing else is going on. And then I'm going to need you take some blood to send out for lab work so we can eliminate any other possibilities." Kerry jotted down some quick notes. "Who's your physician?"

"Dr. Lourdes Fisher." I grimaced, thinking of the handouts Dr. Fisher had given me.

"I'm going to send her a copy of this report. You'll need to schedule an appointment—for as soon as possible—you're going to need a follow-up, as well as the labs. She might want to put you on medication or monitor you."

I narrowed my eyes at Kerry, who I'd liked up until this point. "Great."

She sat down on the floor and regarded me. "A panic attack is no joke, and it's nothing to be embarrassed about. They can sometimes lead to serious complications, so it's good someone called 9-1-1."

"I'm still embarrassed."

Kerry smiled. "Don't be. This is nothing. I got a call earlier today—I had to go cut a guy out of his kitchen. He got a piercing *down there*"—she motioned to her private parts—"and he was making himself breakfast naked because this is Northern California, and people are *weird*. His piercing got stuck on a cabinet hinge when he reached up to get his flour sifter, to sift flour for his pancakes. *No lie.* I had to cut him loose with a pair of wire cutters." She giggled.

In spite of myself, I giggled, too.

"Are you feeling better?" Wes called from outside the door. "Do you need anything?"

Kerry got up and motioned for him. "You can come back in, and I'll check Hannah again in a few minutes." She turned to me. "Would you feel more comfortable in your bed, not on the bathroom floor?"

I started to get up.

"Whoa," Kerry said, "take it easy."

Wes was beside me in an instant. "I got her."

He led me to the bed, and I realized that not only did I feel better, I almost felt normal, as if nothing had happened.

And then I realized Wes was helping *me*. "You need to take it easy," I mumbled.

He shook his head, ignoring what I said.

Kerry ushered the other paramedics to the hallway. "I'll be out here if you need me."

Wes tucked me into the bed and sat down. "Do you feel better?"

"Yeah. I don't think I need to be in bed."

His look told me not to budge.

"I'm *fine*," I insisted. "In fact, I'm living proof that you can't die of embarrassment."

Wes put his hand over mine. "I'm sure that was hard for you, but you have *nothing* to be embarrassed about. I've had guys on my team—men who weigh two-thirty and seem like they could crush a small car with their fists—deal with panic attacks that have incapacitated them. It's a medical emergency. Your body is completely out of your control when it happens, and it's *scary*."

"I don't know why. I was just blow-drying my hair."

"What were you thinking about?"

My shoulders sagged. "The Pace girls. And then it just sort of spiraled. I was thinking about all the things I try not to think about."

"Like?" Wes's voice was gentle.

"Like my parents' car accident. Like when you got shot in front of me."

He winced. "Anything else?"

"Just…violent things. Sad things. Li Na things." I squeezed his hand. "She deserves to pay for what she's done, you know. I can't stop thinking about it."

Wes's gaze held mine. "Me, either."

"I don't know what we can do."

"We'll figure something out," Wes said, his voice gentle. "But I think we need to talk about what's going on with you."

Kerry knocked on the door and stuck her head in. "Are you ready for me?"

"Sure," I said, eager for the interruption.

Wes patted my hand. "We'll talk more later."

"Maybe not today," Kerry said, ushering him out of the way. "Hannah needs to rest."

I'd never be able to tell her, but Kerry might just be my new favorite person.

Chapter 11

WES

"Why didn't you tell me before?" I asked Brian.

He shoved his hands into his pockets. "I don't know, but she specifically asked me not to tell you that she was going to see her doctor. Which is why I knew I needed to."

I went and stood by the windows. "I don't know why she'd want to keep something from me."

Brian scratched his head. "Maybe she doesn't want you to worry? You do sort of worry a lot—and hover. You've been hovering."

"Not *my* little brother," a voice I'd know anywhere boomed.

I turned. "Ellis?"

My big brother grinned at me from the middle of Gabe and Lauren's kitchen. "Levi said I'd find you here."

He shook Brian's hand, then came over, pulling me in for a quick hug. If I was a big guy, Ellis was a huge one. He was six foot four and thickly muscled. It felt like being hugged by a large boulder.

"You look good, buddy," he said, examining me. "No more wheelchair?"

"I'm done with it."

"You got cleared?"

"I sort of cleared myself."

Ellis patted me on the shoulder in full-on big-brother mode. "Sounds about right. How're you feeling?"

"I'm better. I'm going back to see Dr. Kim, and I'm hoping to get the green light to go back to work."

Beneath his buzz cut, Ellis's eyebrow arched a fraction. "Seems a little early, doesn't it?"

"Didn't you just retire?" I asked him.

"Yeah. So?"

"Seems a little early for that, too."

Brian coughed. "I'll see you guys later."

Ellis looked around. "Where is everybody? How's Hannah?"

"She's not good—she just had a panic attack. The paramedics left here an hour ago."

"Is she okay?"

"Yes. No. I don't know. She's sleeping."

Concern etched Ellis's face—he adored Hannah. "What happened?"

"Did you hear about Jim Pace?"

"Levi caught me up. I called him on my way over here." He sounded grim. "We believe Li Na Zhao is responsible, correct?"

I nodded. "We'll have a hell of a time proving it, but yes. Hannah's friends with his wife. The whole thing's hitting her hard, especially since she hasn't had a chance to fully recover from being kidnapped."

"Jesus." Ellis flopped down on one of the enormous leather couches. "Zhao's terrorizing Silicon Valley. She wanted to buy the wife's company, right? The one that's developing the anti-cancer therapy?"

I grabbed us each a glass of water and sat on the couch directly across from him. "From what I understand, yes. And she's also started trying to hack Lauren again."

Ellis gripped his glass. "I guess I came back at the right time—I won't be bored."

"About that. I want you to have the house. I'm going to get a new place, for when Hannah and I are back on our feet and ready to move out of here."

Ellis's eyes sparkled with interest. He was a macho marine, but he still loved to gossip. "You're moving in together?"

"Uh… Not exactly." I should've thought it through before I brought it up to Ellis. *You should've at least mentioned it to Hannah before anyone else, dumbass.*

Ellis arched his eyebrow again, clearly enjoying my discomfort. "You're 'not exactly' moving in together?"

"Uh." *Why did I open my big mouth?*

"If you're buying a house for her, you should probably figure it out," Ellis teased. "But I hope it works out—I like Hannah. I think my baby brother's finally found someone our mother would approve of."

"Mom would love her," I agreed. At least I could say *that* with some authority.

"She totally would."

I leaned back against the supple leather of the couch, but I couldn't get close to relaxing, so I decided to turn the tables. "What about you? Are you ready to meet someone and finally settle down now that you're a civilian?"

"I'm not the settling-down kind. You know that."

I grinned. "You should know that Hannah's going to try to find you a girlfriend—she's already plotting."

He spluttered, practically choking on his water. "I hope you're kidding."

I held my hands up as if in surrender. "Take it up with her. I'm not responsible for her actions."

Ellis's phone buzzed, and he grabbed it. "It's Levi—I gotta go. I guess I'm officially on duty."

"I'm glad you're back."

He smiled as he hopped to his feet. "Me, too. But warn Hannah: no girlfriends. I'm not interested in dating one of her sorority sisters."

I just shook my head as I watched him go. The poor bastard had no idea what he was up against when Hannah Taylor set her mind to something.

I couldn't wait to watch him figure that out.

* * *

"We don't have to go," Lauren told Hannah, for the second time.

Hannah looked up from her steel-cut oatmeal, sprinkled with berries and flaxseed, which she'd hardly touched. "I already told you I'm going. Fiona needs our support. I'm not skipping the service just because you're worried about me."

Lauren reached across the table and took Hannah's hand. "You had something very scary happen to you yesterday. There's no reason to minimize it, and there's also no reason to push yourself."

Hannah yanked her hand away and got up from the table. "I'm not pushing myself—I'm living. I love you, and I know you're worried about me, but please stop driving me crazy! I'm going to get dressed." She hustled off before Lauren could object.

Lauren put her face in her hands. "I don't want to push, but I am seriously worried about her."

"I know. I'm taking her to see Dr. Fisher later for a follow-up. I'll make sure we find out exactly what's going on and what we need to do."

"Thank you."

As I stood to leave, Lauren said, "Wes? With everything that's happened, I haven't asked how *you* are. Are you okay? It's great to see you out of the wheelchair, but I want to make sure you aren't pushing yourself. And yes, I do realize I sound like a broken record."

"I'm fine. After we see Dr. Fisher, we're headed to see Dr. Kim—hopefully, I'll get a clean bill of health."

Lauren bit her lip. "I want to ask you for something, but I know I'm overstepping."

"Is it an overstep that protects your sister?"

"Yes."

"Then I'm in," I said immediately.

"Would you consider asking her to go talk to someone?"

"A therapist?"

Lauren nodded.

I'd thought the same thing. "Yes, but I don't know if she'd be open to it."

"Would you offer to…go with her? You've both been through a lot."

Therapy was not my idea of a good time, but I would do anything for Hannah—even if it involved talking about my feelings in front of a complete stranger. "If you think it'll help, I'll go."

Lauren's shoulders sagged in relief. "Thank you. I know it's silly for you two to go to couples' therapy, but I think that's the only way she'll agree."

I bobbled at her words. "Why's it silly?"

"Well, it's not as if you two were really serious before all this happened. Couples' therapy is usually for people in long-term, committed relationships."

Her words cut me. Apparently, I wasn't considered long-term potential—I guess they thought of me as more like the hired help. *Who doesn't read.* "Oh. I see."

She blinked at me—Lauren wasn't the most socially astute person, but she could tell she'd said something wrong. "I just mean, it's generous of you to offer to go."

"Uh-huh." I backed away before I did something stupid, like ask if Hannah had told her we weren't serious. "We're all going to the service in the same car this morning, right?"

"I have to go to Paragon afterwards, so Gabe and I will meet you there." Lauren looked at me pleadingly. "Will you please make sure she's okay to handle this? I know she doesn't want me bugging her, but it's going to be very emotional."

"Of course I will. I promise, I'm looking out for her." I could at least promise that.

"I know. And Wes?"

"Yes?"

"Thank you. For everything."

* * *

"I already told you—I'm not going to talk about it." Hannah adjusted the pink shawl she wore over her black dress. "Not this morning."

"Fine." But it wasn't fine, and I was still reeling from the back-to-back conversations I'd had with our respective siblings.

Me to Ellis: I'm going to ask Hannah to move in with me.

Lauren to me: Couples' therapy is for 'real' couples, but you're so sweet for being a placeholder and helping out!

Hannah sighed. "I don't want to fight with you. I'm too tired to fight."

We sat in the backseat as the driver maneuvered the car up in front of the Unitarian Universalist church in Palo Alto. From the passenger seat, Brian watched the crowd waiting outside to go inside to Jim Pace's service. He let out a low whistle. "There's a lot of people here."

I looked at Hannah. "I don't want to fight, either—but are you *sure* you're up for this?"

She peered out the window. "Fiona needs our support."

I shoved all the other thoughts away—they could wait for later. Hannah needed me, and that was the most important thing. I laced my fingers through hers. "Then let's go."

As soon as we were out of the car, I noticed the agents from Betts Security—they were everywhere. Levi was taking no chances at this event. I counted at least nine undercover agents before we even made it through the entrance of the church, in addition to Brian, who followed right behind us.

Hannah stayed close as we made our way up the line. She looked beautiful and completely pulled together. No one would guess that twelve hours ago, she'd had a panic attack so vicious, she'd required emergency medical attention. The procession snaked slowly toward the receiving line, and I kept my arm secured firmly around her waist.

"Is that *Ellis*?" she asked, peering over my shoulder.

"Where?" But I answered my own question as I turned. My brother was standing behind Fiona Pace, scrutinizing every person who stopped to offer their condolences. "I guess she's his new assignment."

"Wow. I guess Levi really *was* impressed with him."

A stupid throb of jealousy ran through me. *I need to get back to work.* "Ellis is amazing, and he's a total pro. He'll keep Fiona safe."

Hannah squeezed my hand. "I know. And I'm sure you're anxious to get back out there, but stay with me, big guy." She leaned back against my chest. "I need you."

My heart squeezed. "I'm right here. I've got you, and I'm not letting go." I kept my arm wrapped firmly around her, emotions battling inside me.

We finally made it to the front of the line, and Fiona immediately reached for Hannah. "I'm so glad you're here. Thank you."

"This is Wesley."

We shook hands, and Fiona smiled at me warmly, then Hannah enveloped her in a hug.

"How are you holding up? How are the girls?" Hannah asked.

"I'm…dealing. And the girls are with my mom, playing in the children's room. I might let them stay back there…"

Fiona turned to me. "Wesley, it's so nice to finally meet you. I've heard wonderful things."

"I'm so sorry about Jim." I hugged her, too. "I'm glad to see my brother is on your detail. He's the best. He'll keep your family safe."

"Ellis mentioned you were brothers." She pulled back and wiped her eyes. "He doesn't talk much, does he?"

I chuckled as Ellis's steely gaze flicked to me—he must have overheard her. "No, he doesn't. It's actually sort of nice."

Ellis gave me a dirty look, which I ignored.

The group of people behind us moved closer, so Fiona excused herself after giving Hannah another hug.

The service was about to begin when Gabe and Lauren slid into the pew next to us.

"What took you so long?" Hannah asked. We'd all been about to leave the house at the same time.

Gabe and Lauren looked at each other briefly.

"There was some work stuff we had to take care of," Gabe said, his tone neutral.

Lauren didn't say anything. She looked down, playing with her engagement ring.

"What sort of stuff?" Hannah asked, immediately on alert.

Before Gabe could answer, the service started, and he turned away. I thought he seemed relieved not to have to talk.

Hannah looked at me, her brow furrowed with worry. I squeezed her hand, wishing I could soothe her. Something was going on with Gabe and Lauren—they were hiding something. But we were at a funeral, and that seemed like more than enough to deal with for one morning.

Chapter 12

HANNAH

I pulled out my compact and put some concealer underneath my eyes. My mascara had run at the service, and I didn't want Dr. Fisher to pounce on me for crying. "They didn't have to say it. *Of course* it had something to do with Li Na. Otherwise they wouldn't have been looking at each other like that, and then they ran out of there—"

Wes sighed. "Just because Gabe and Lauren had to leave before we could ask them what happened does *not* mean it's about Li Na. Not necessarily."

I stared at him until he gave in.

"Okay, something's definitely up, but we'll talk to them tonight, okay? We don't need to drive ourselves crazy right now."

I snapped my compact shut. "Crazy. That's the perfect word choice."

Wes put his hand over mine. "Having a panic attack doesn't make you crazy. With everything that's happened, it'd be crazier if you *didn't* have one."

"*You* haven't had one."

"I was unconscious while you were kidnapped. Trust me, I would've had a panic attack if I'd known, if not worse."

I twisted my ponytail, nervous about seeing Dr. Fisher. The driver pulled up alongside the curb in front of her practice, and I frowned. "She's going to say 'I told you so.' I know it."

"Why?" Wes asked.

"Never mind." I shook my head. "I'm just babbling."

Wes looked like he wanted to ask more, but he bit his questions back as we went inside to wait. When the nurse came out to the waiting room, she said, "Dr. Fisher is ready for you. She'd like to speak with both of you, actually."

Wes didn't look at me, probably knowing I'd object. We followed the nurse into an exam room, and Dr. Fisher came in a moment later. She introduced herself to Wesley and then turned to me. "I read the report in your file—I'm sorry you went through that. The good news is, your labs came back normal. That's great."

"Good." In the back of my overactive-imagination-prone mind, I'd been worried I had some rare form of cancer that manifested itself in panic attacks.

She began examining me, listening to my heart and taking my blood pressure as Wes watched carefully.

"What's her blood pressure?" he asked.

Dr. Fisher smiled. "One-ten over sixty. It's perfect."

"Good." Wes sounded relieved. He seemed to know a lot more about medicine than I did, even though I devoutly watched *Grey's Anatomy* and had previously believed that qualified me as somewhat of an expert.

"Does everything look okay?" he asked Dr. Fisher once she'd finished checking my pulse and staring into my eyes with an annoying light.

She smiled again—apparently, she liked Wes and his never-ending list of medical questions. "Her vitals are completely normal."

Wes grinned. "That's a relief."

Dr. Fisher wrote down some notes. When she turned around, she said, "Why don't you both come to my office? I have some things I'd like to discuss with you."

I stiffened. "Um, no offense, Dr. Fisher, but isn't having Wesley in my appointment a HIPAA violation?"

"You recently listed him as your emergency contact," she reminded me.

She was getting on my nerves again. "Is this an emergency?"

"Not yet. But what happened to you last night qualifies as one." She gave me a long look. "Would you agree to grant him permission to join us?"

I glanced at Wes. "I guess so."

After Dr. Fisher left, I stood and grabbed my things, waiting for Wesley to excuse himself from my appointment. When he didn't, I put my hands on my hips. "Why are you in here?"

He looked down at his shoes. "I…called the doctor this morning. And asked if we could both meet with her."

"Wes. Look at me."

He looked up, but his expression wasn't as guilty as I'd hoped.

"I'm worried about you, and since you're not sharing details, I thought it would be a good idea if I met with Dr. Fisher." His chin was set stubbornly. "I need to hear what she has to say about this—if you need help, I want to give it to you."

"That's sweet, but you don't have the right—"

"I'm asking you for the right. Begging, actually." He came over and wrapped his arms around my waist. "I'm not trying to get all in your business or be controlling. I just want you to be safe."

He kissed the top of my head, and I groaned. I didn't want him here, but I felt good in his arms—safe, secure, and utterly protected. I wanted to argue with him, but I felt too loved.

It was official: I was getting spoiled, all soft and spongy because he kept taking care of me and being all hot, sexy, and protective.

Where's my damned checklist?

"Fine. But I think you should have asked my permission before you crashed my appointment."

"Would you have let me come?"

"No," I admitted.

"If it gets too personal and you want me to leave, I promise I will. But if she wants to talk about precautions we can take to prevent anxiety and panic attacks, and things we need to look out for, I want to be part of the conversation. Do I have permission for that?"

He leaned down and kissed me, and I had that feeling again. Safe. Warm. *Worshipped.* I should be pushing him away right now, punishing him for overstepping boundaries, but I just wanted to pull him closer. *Grr.*

"Okay. But let's get this over with."

* * *

WES

Hannah wouldn't look at me as the driver took us across town to my appointment at El Camino.

I put my hand gently over hers. "Going to couples' therapy is not the end of the world, you know."

"Maybe not, but the fact that Lauren called Dr. Fisher and asked her to refer us to a therapist? *That* might be the end of the world." Hannah shook her head. "Just wait till I get my hands on her."

"She's worried about you—she's just trying to help." I remembered Lauren's words again from this morning and my stomach turned, but I ignored it.

"Butting in on my business—*our* business—is not helping."

"Hannah?" I waited until she turned to me. "I told Lauren it was okay. She asked me if I thought it was a good idea this morning. I said I didn't know, but that if it would help, we should try."

"I'm tired of you all ganging up on me." She tilted her chin, looking extremely annoyed. "I'm *fine*. I feel like I should just get a T-shirt that says that, so you'll all leave me be." She shook her head and went back to staring out the window.

I had a strong sense of déjà vu when, twenty minutes later, Dr. Kim's nurse asked Hannah to join my appointment. Hannah looked pleased as she settled herself onto a chair in the examination room, watching as the nurse asked me routine questions and took my vitals.

When she'd finished doing intake, the nurse grabbed her laptop and headed for the door. "Dr. Kim will be in in just a minute."

"I didn't call him," Hannah said as soon as we were alone.

I grimaced. "Maybe your sister did."

That made her smile. "Maybe."

Dr. Kim came in. "Hello, Hannah." His face split into a grin when he saw me. "Good morning. Wesley, you look good!"

"Thank you, Dr. Kim. I've been working hard."

Dr. Kim flipped through my file, reviewing some notes. "That's what your physical therapist says."

"She's tough. Did she actually say something nice about me? Because I thought she might be trying to kill me."

"She said you're handling therapy well." He laughed, then did a quick inventory of the room. "No wheelchair today?"

I looked at Hannah and quickly turned away. "I haven't been using it for the past couple of days. I don't think I need it anymore."

Dr. Kim folded his long, lean runner's body down to sit on a rolling stool. He tapped his chin with his pen, considering me. "Did your physical therapist tell you it was okay to go without the wheelchair?"

I could feel Hannah staring at me. "Not exactly."

"Did the cardiologist clear you to walk?"

I scratched my head.

"Your orthopedic doctor?"

I coughed.

Dr. Kim tapped his pen. "So, you just decided to take matters into your own hands?"

"It was time. I felt strong enough, and I haven't had any issues. Have I, honey?"

Hannah scowled at me, her arms crossed against her chest.

Dr. Kim turned to her. "Has he been getting around okay, Hannah?"

"He's doing better than I expected," she admitted.

"Well, let's run some tests," Dr. Kim said. "If everything checks out cognitively, you might very well graduate today."

"Graduate to what?" I sounded hopeful to my own ears.

Dr. Kim held up his hand. "I'm not making any promises. Let's see how you're doing first."

"I'm ready to go back to work," I insisted as Dr. Kim came toward me with his annoying light to shine in my eyes.

"Listen to the doctor," Hannah insisted.

Right before the light got shoved into my eyes, I looked at her. "Only if you listen to yours."

She rolled her eyes. "Fine."

"Fine." But if Dr. Kim said no work, I wasn't going to be fine. Not for much longer. The icing on the cake was Hannah's panic attack last night, followed by Jim Pace's funeral this morning.

I was done with the waiting.

Chapter 13

WES

"Are you really going to look for a new place?" Gabe motioned to the patio we were sitting at, his glorious lawn stretching out all around us. "All this isn't enough for you?"

I chuckled. "I love it here—but now that Ellis is back, I want him to have my house. I hope it's okay if I stay until then."

"We want you here. It's safer, and quite frankly, you're much nicer to have around than Levi. You can stay forever, as far as we're concerned."

"Thanks, buddy. That means a lot."

His kind words didn't stop me from wincing at the thought of being separated from Hannah, or from frowning at my dinner. I pushed the tofu around with my fork.

"What's the matter, bean curd doesn't excite you?" Gabe joked.

"Do we *ever* get to eat meat again?" I kept my voice low, hoping Lauren and Hannah couldn't hear me from the kitchen.

Gabe speared a pale rectangle of tofu and inspected it. "Let's go to the steakhouse Friday night. I'll ask my brothers to come—ask Ellis, too. Guys' night."

"I am so in."

Lauren and Hannah came out to the patio. I forced myself to smile and simultaneously willed my stomach to hold down the slimy tofu. *Jesus, do people actually think this is good?*

Hannah patted my hand. "You're such a good sport with your vegan meal, honey."

I coughed. "It's good. Really good."

Gabe started laughing, and Lauren rolled her eyes at him. "Remember when we started dating? You stopped eating red meat to be supportive."

"I was trying to get you into my *bed*." He reached out and put his hand possessively over hers. "Now we're engaged, babe. We're in for better or for worse territory." He held up an offending piece of tofu. "This is the 'worse' part. The steak is the 'better' part—better because I get to eat it again, and you can't run away from me, because you'd have to take me to court."

Lauren giggled. I'd worked for her for two years, and I'd never heard her laugh before she met Gabe.

Then her phone buzzed, and she jumped up. "It's Leo—I need to take this."

Lauren spoke to him for only a minute, but when she hung up, she looked pale. "Li Na hacked into our system again just now. I have to get to the lab."

"Is this what you weren't telling me at Jim's service—she's been in the server again?" Hannah glared.

"I thought you were dealing with enough for one morning." Lauren grabbed her plate, and Gabe and Hannah both got up to follow her. "No—you two stay here. Depending on what the damage is, I might need you both tomorrow for a planning session. I'll find out what she's up to, and then we'll take action. Okay?"

Gabe and Hannah both frowned, and Lauren frowned right back, not bothering to coddle them. "I won't be long." She left before they could argue further.

Gabe looked as if he'd like to smash something. "I don't know what the hell Li Na's doing now."

"I don't, either," Hannah said. "Lauren and I were just talking about it—what could she be after? She knows Lauren won't sell. She's already seen most of the proprietary information."

"And she's busy terrorizing Fiona Pace into selling her company," I finished. I cringed, thinking of how frail Fiona had looked at the service this morning, how devastated she was about her husband.

Hannah looked to Gabe. "Lauren said you have a theory about Li Na and what she's after. I don't understand how she could do these things—have people kidnapped and murdered—just for money."

Gabe scrubbed a hand across his face. "It's not just for the money. Money would be too easy, and Li Na already has plenty of it."

"So why is she doing these terrible things? To get *ahead*?"

Gabe shoved his plate away. "It's along those lines, but it's more complicated. Have you had any experience dealing with Chinese business partners before?"

"No," Hannah said. "Paragon hasn't really started a comprehensive marketing campaign there yet."

Gabe leaned toward me. "Wes? You have some expertise, don't you?"

"My military foreign-relations background focused on China." I shrugged. "Ellis and I have both been there several times on assignment, so I know something about the culture."

Hannah's jaw dropped. "You don't tell me *anything*."

"It never came up." I nudged her, then focused back on Gabe. "What were you saying?"

"My theory on Li Na is that she's after 'face'—it's a Chinese sociological concept. In Chinese business, 'face' is extremely important. It's your social and business standing, your social currency, your level of respect, honor, and worth. Respect is crucial in corporate China."

I put down the offensive tofu, giving up on dinner. "And Li Na insists she has her government's backing, correct?"

"That's right." Gabe nodded. "She's said repeatedly that she's helping to invigorate the city of Shenzhen and that her country would never extradite her."

Hannah leaned forward. "Tell me more about 'face'—I want to understand exactly what it means."

"This requires reinforcements." Gabe went and grabbed three beers from the fridge. Hannah scowled as I opened mine.

"I'm cleared for everything except work," I reminded her, and winked.

Her face reddened.

Gabe wrapped his fingers tightly around his beer. "When we were looking for ammunition against her, before the closing, I dug a little deeper into Jiàn Innovations. I realized that Li Na's been making promises for some time about the great things her company's going to do, and all the prestige they're going to bring to Shenzhen. To date, she's failed to follow through. She couldn't get the patch, and Jiàn's market reach hasn't grown much outside of China."

I took a sip of beer. "She's getting desperate."

Gabe looked thoughtful. "Seems like it. She didn't even try to bargain with Fiona Pace—she just went straight to murder."

Hannah put her face in her hands, and I wrapped my arm around her. "It's okay."

"Sorry," Gabe said.

"You two don't have to apologize. Li Na's the one with blood on her hands." She peered out from above her fingers. "We need to go after her. I know you don't want to kill her, but I don't see how we can extricate ourselves from this situation without making her go away permanently."

"I agree," I said. "We need to get rid of her. I'm sure Hannah doesn't want to hear this right now, but Ellis and I both have the military training perfect for a situation like this."

"Wes, *no*."

I rubbed her back. "What you said is true—she needs to be dealt with, once and for all."

"We're not risking you and Ellis," Gabe said. "We have to figure something else out."

"But while we put it through a committee and try to be ethical and conscientious, Fiona and her girls are grieving the loss of a good man. It's not right." Hannah took a sip of beer. "Li Na needs to be dealt with—I'm done being afraid all the time. Screw ethical and conscientious."

"What are you proposing?" Gabe asked.

"Nothing that involves Wesley or Ellis, that's for sure."

I put my hand on hers. "Baby—"

"Don't 'baby' me!" she barked. "You almost died this year. That's enough risk for me for one lifetime, thank you. We're moving forward. Not dying."

"What are we going to do if we don't go after her?" I asked.

Hannah rubbed her temples. "Let me think about it."

* * *

HANNAH

Wesley had insisted on walking four miles on the treadmill before we went to bed. I sat and watched, a wreck, as sweat poured off him.

"This is frickin' humiliating," he said, wiping himself down with a towel and breathing hard.

"You have nothing to be embarrassed about." I followed him back upstairs when he'd finished. "And you don't have to push yourself so hard."

"I'm not interested in continuing my career as an invalid, thank you very much. I've done my time."

"You just walked four miles, and you haven't used your wheelchair all week." I tugged on his arm. "You're not an invalid, and there's nothing wrong with taking the time to heal!"

He grunted, heading for the bathroom.

I paced our room, waiting for him to get out of the shower. Lauren texted me, saying things were under control at Paragon. She promised to be home early. We needed to discuss strategy tomorrow—about how to deal with Li Na going forward.

But I didn't want to just "deal" with Li Na. I longed to see her face-to-face so I could punch her. I was pretty good in my cardio-kickboxing class—I yearned to land a nice, hard kick to her face, to do some damage to those high cheekbones of hers.

But she wasn't here, and I couldn't kick her, and I sure as hell couldn't let Wes go to Shenzhen to kill her.

Wes. He continued to surprise me. First the fact that he'd read Fiona's book, then the fact that he had a background in foreign relations with China. I'd underestimated him, which made me sort of an asshole.

He'd also been there for me during the panic attack, when I woke up from my nightmares, and when I'd had to face my doctor. He kept showing up, and he kept making me feel like I was worth showing up for.

Wes was *so* not going to Shenzhen.

He came out of the bathroom then, a towel wrapped around his waist, and I sucked in a breath. We hadn't talked about any bedroom issues for a while, but Dr. Kim had cleared him for sexual intercourse today. "Just don't get too crazy," the doctor had joked.

My cheeks burned as Wes stalked through the room, obviously still pissed about sweating so much from his walk. "I think I'm ready for bed—I'm tired from my walk."

He said "walk" as though it were something disgusting he'd found on the bottom of his shoe.

"You can't be so hard on yourself—it'll just make the whole process feel like it's taking longer. You're doing great. Even Dr. Kim thinks so."

He rolled his eyes and let the towel drop to the floor as he grabbed some boxer briefs from his drawer.

I sucked in another breath as I inspected him…every inch of him. Had he gotten *bigger*? Or had it just been a really long time?

"Babe?"

I jerked my gaze away from his naked parts. "Yeah?"

He grinned. "Are you staring at my dick?"

I tried not to notice it was growing. "N-no."

He pulled his underwear up. "I'll just put it away, then."

"You don't have to." I licked my lips and tried to gather my courage. "Dr. Kim said you were okay to…*you know*."

Wes pulled a T-shirt over his head, then smiled at me. "That doesn't mean we have to do it tonight."

I felt crestfallen and relieved all at the same time. "Don't you want to?"

He laughed, then shrugged. "Of course I want to. But I want the time to be right, for both of us."

But the time *was* right for him—finally. I was fine. I could do this.

I went and tentatively wrapped my arms around him, relishing the feel of his muscles against me. He might not be back to where he was before the injury, but it felt like he was regaining strength fast.

I sighed in relief.

"What?" His question came out muffled against my hair.

"You feel like you're getting stronger, back to your old self. I'm just so relieved."

He held me tighter. "Shh, I got you."

My body throbbed for his. It had been *so* long. "I want you to make love to me." I reached up to kiss him.

His tongue sought mine, and I moaned against him. He ran his hands down my back, pulling me closer, and my body molded against his.

My body continued to respond, but I couldn't fully focus. My thoughts kept crowding me. *I want him. I want to do this.*

Ugh, I willed my brain, *then shut up!*

Wes deepened the kiss, and I wrapped my hands around his hips, getting as close to him as possible. I tried to lose myself in his embrace, but I wondered what he was thinking right now, if I felt the same to him as I always had...

His hands roamed through my hair, and I stiffened. *I want him. I want to do this. I can do this...* He kissed me again, but I felt like I was two seconds behind, trying to catch up and not connecting to the moment.

He pulled back. "Are you okay?"

I shook my head, trying to clear it. "What do you mean?"

"You seemed like you checked out a little."

"I think I just got distracted."

He brushed the hair back from my face. "Let's just go to bed, okay? I'm beat."

I stepped back, stung. "I didn't mean to ruin the mood. Can't we just forget about it—"

"Hey." He reached out and grabbed my hand. "We are in no rush. C'mon, we're both tired. It's been a long day."

"I'll just be a minute." My voice came out small.

I retreated to the bathroom with my pajamas. I changed and started brushing my teeth, staring at myself in the mirror. There were dark circles under my eyes. My complexion looked dull. I barely resembled my normal, perky self.

I was tired. I was tired of this shit.

I roughly pulled my pajama top on and headed to bed. I climbed in and faced away from Wes.

He sat up a little and sighed. "You're mad at me? I wasn't trying to be a jerk."

"You weren't a jerk."

He was quiet for a minute. "I just don't want to rush you."

"I'm perfectly capable of deciding what I'm ready for, thank you very much." I sounded meaner than I felt.

He sighed again and lay back down. "I know that. But you hesitated."

"So?"

"*So* there was no way in hell I was going to keep going if you were just going through the motions—or worse, you were doing it for *me*."

"I wasn't going through the motions—like I said, I got distracted for a second." I swallowed hard. "And I wasn't doing it just for you. I miss having sex, too, you know."

Wes sighed again. "That doesn't mean we have to rush it."

"It doesn't mean we have to wait until it's perfect either." Part of me just wanted to get it over with.

"Of course not." He rolled over and put his arms around me.

I relaxed against his warmth, even as different emotions jostled inside me.

He was quiet for so long, I'd thought he'd fallen asleep, but then he said, "What distracted you?"

"I couldn't stop…thinking."

"About what?"

"Just thinking. That I wanted to do it, that the way we were kissing felt good."

"You had to convince yourself?" Even though it was a loaded question, Wes only sounded genuinely curious.

"It wasn't that. It was more like I was waiting for myself to freak out, and I was trying to head it off."

He played with my hair. "Why were you worried you were going to freak out?"

I sighed. "I had a panic attack last night, remember? I'm not exactly in control of my emotions right now."

Wesley dropped the lock of hair he'd been twisting. He sat up. "But what does that have to do with us being intimate?"

"I don't know! It's emotional, I guess. I was worried I'd react weird." My half-truths were confusing me as much as him.

Wes sighed. "I want you to know that I'm not judging you—I hope I don't sound defensive, because that's not what this is about."

I wrapped my arms around myself. "I know that. Listen, let's talk about this another time, because tomorrow's another hellish day. We have to meet with Lauren at Paragon about this newest round of hacking."

"And I made us an appointment with the couples' therapist Dr. Fisher recommended. It's for first thing tomorrow morning."

I'd thought Wes agreed with me about seeing the therapist—and didn't want to go. "What? Why'd you do that?"

"Because we've both been through a lot." He patted my back kindly, but in a way that also made it clear he wouldn't budge an inch.

"I don't need to see a therapist, and I don't have time."

"Do it for me, then. Just come with me to the first appointment."

I cursed inwardly, wishing we'd just had stupid sex and gotten it over with. I'd be fine once we did, I knew it.

"Fine," I said.

"Fine," he said back.

But I wondered if we really were. Fine, I meant.

Chapter 14

WES

Hannah didn't say a word on the way to the therapist's office in Cupertino. She twisted the hem of her dress nervously and bounced her knee.

"You don't need to fidget." I put my hand over hers. "This is going to be low-key."

"Really? Have you ever been before?"

She didn't mention that we were going to see a psychotherapist—Brian and the driver were close enough to hear.

"No," I admitted. "Have you?"

She sighed. "I went after my parents died, just for a few months."

"Did it help?"

"It was intense."

"We can handle intense." But I was dreading the appointment, too. As a former marine who'd had several active tours of duty, I had a pretty extensive list of shit I never wanted to think about.

I hoped we wouldn't have to go there.

I was doing this for Hannah. I'd promised Lauren, and even though I had mixed feelings about my conversation with her, a promise was a promise. As such, I couldn't really whine about seeing a highly recommended, five-hundred-dollar-per-hour doctor.

Dr. Katherine McGovern was probably going to stick us on a modern, uncomfortable couch in a room filled with potted plants and ask us about our feelings. If I could survive a gunshot wound, a head injury, and a medically induced coma, I could probably deal with an hour of therapy.

I hoped.

Hannah laced her fingers through mine as I opened the car door. "I'm pretty sure I'm mad at you about this," she said.

"Okay. But we're still going."

She groaned as I pulled her into the lobby, Brian following close behind. It felt weird having a security guard, but at the same time, it helped me relax—a little.

If anyone wanted Hannah, they would have to go through me *and* Brian first.

I greeted the receptionist, a young woman with a pierced nose and purple hair. "Wesley Eden and Hannah Taylor, for Dr. McGovern."

She smiled warmly from behind the desk. "Dr. Kathy will be out in just a minute."

"Dr. Kathy," aka Katherine McGovern, MD, graduate of Yale School of Medicine, came out a few moments later. She was short, with corkscrew-curly hair, lavender-framed cat-eye glasses, a rumpled denim dress, and clogs. She looked more like a kindergarten teacher than a physician. She smiled, motioning for us to follow her.

Kathy ushered us into her office, and I peered around—instead of a modern couch with clean lines, there was a slightly dilapidated love seat and two overstuffed chairs. There were some plants, but the room was dominated by an overflow of books, piled on every available space.

"Would you like some water? Tea?" Kathy asked, so kindly that I worried she might ask to hug us.

"No, thank you." Hannah smiled politely.

"Thanks for fitting us in this morning," I said. "Dr. Fisher highly recommended you."

"Lourdes and I went to medical school together," Kathy said. She sat back in her chair. "Now, why don't you two tell me why you're here?"

"Wesley was injured, and he's having a hard time with rehab. He doesn't like taking it slow," Hannah tattled.

I grimaced. "Hannah was kidnapped, and she had a panic attack two nights ago. We had to call the paramedics."

Hannah gave me a dirty look, then immediately composed her features.

I did the same thing right back at her.

"How long have you two been a couple?" Kathy asked, unruffled.

I shrugged. "Six months, give or take the month I was in the hospital."

"Are you married?" the doctor asked.

"No," Hannah said. "We live together—right now we're staying at my sister's house for security reasons. It's a long story."

Kathy nodded. "Tell me the five-minute version so we can focus on what's really going on here."

Hannah and I took turns explaining about Li Na Zhao, Paragon, and what happened when I was shot and Hannah was taken prisoner.

"So…you two are only living together out of convenience, for safety purposes?" Dr. Kathy asked.

"No," Hannah said.

"Yes," I said at the same time.

Hannah looked at me sharply. "That's the only reason?"

I could feel my face redden as both she and the doctor watched me. "Uh…"

"What will you do when the safety threat passes?" the doctor asked.

"I'm buying a new house." I smoothed my pants, which were already smooth. "I sort of just gave my brother my old one."

I was going to ask Hannah to move in with me, but her sister made me feel like a moron.

"Let's change direction for a moment," Kathy said, letting me off the hook. "I want to talk more about what happened. Where were you held when these men had you?" Kathy asked Hannah.

"We were in Oakland, only I didn't know that until afterward. They never let me outside."

"What other sort of rules did they have for you?"

Hannah looked taken aback that the doctor was talking about this so soon. "Uh, nothing, really."

Kathy waited, watching her.

"They just kept me in a room. They didn't feed me much or talk to me. They let me watch television, though, which was good. I think I would've gone crazy without *General Hospital*."

Hannah smiled at the doctor, but the doctor didn't smile back.

"What else did they let you do?" she asked.

"I got to Skype my sister a few times. And they let me have vodka once or twice." Her face reddened slightly.

"Hold that thought." Kathy turned to me. "Wesley? What about you? What have you been struggling with?"

"It's been hard not being able to work," I admitted. "And I didn't like feeling like I couldn't take care of myself."

"That's hard for you?"

I shrugged. "My parents are both dead. I'm a marine. I'm sort of used to being a lone wolf. But Hannah's been wonderful. She never makes me feel bad or that I'm bothering her when I need something."

"Why would she?" Kathy asked. "You did get shot trying to protect her, after all. She'd be a total bitch if she made you pay for your injuries emotionally, too, don't you think?"

I coughed. "I guess so." It appeared that Kathy, with her clogs and her offers of tea, didn't mince words.

"But I wouldn't do that, and Wes wouldn't be with someone who treated him like that, so it's sort of beside the point," Hannah said.

Kathy smiled at her. "Agreed. But Wesley was praising you for this, and I wanted him to see what he was really doing."

I looked at her, confused. "Um, I'm sorry—what was I really doing?"

The doctor rested her face on her hands. "You were belittling yourself for being a burden."

"I was?"

Hannah reached over and squeezed my hand.

"So, how are things going in the bedroom?" Kathy asked.

I was glad I'd said no to tea—I would've spit it out.

"Nothing like just cutting to the chase, huh?" I asked.

"Couples don't come to me unless they need help. I can usually get a pretty good sense of what sort of help they need, based on what's going on with them in the bedroom. So," she said, smiling again, "what's going on with you two in bed?"

Hannah cleared her throat. "Wes just got approved by his doctor to have sex, but we haven't yet."

"Why not?" Kathy didn't blink.

"We started to fool around last night, but we stopped."

"I was worried she wasn't ready, because she'd just had a panic attack the night before." I shrugged. "I didn't want to rush it."

"You said you started fooling around—what happened? What made you stop, specifically?" Kathy asked.

"I thought Hannah seemed distracted, so I wanted to wait," I said. I could feel my face burning—I'd never talked to someone I didn't know about my sex life before.

Kathy looked to Hannah. "And what did *you* want?"

In response, Hannah scowled.

"Hannah?" Kathy sat back. "I'd like to remind you that honesty is your best shot in here. We gain nothing by wasting each other's time with platitudes. If you waste my time, you're wasting *your* time and Wes's. And you won't get better, and neither will your relationship."

Hannah shot me an *I-told-you-therapy-was-going-to-suck* look.

"So?" Kathy asked. "What did you want last night when you and Wesley were finally fooling around?"

Hannah composed her face. "I wanted to have sex with Wes. But I was thinking too much, and I got distracted by that, and then…then the whole thing sort of got away from me."

"And Wesley noticed." Kathy looked at me approvingly.

"Yes, Wesley noticed," Hannah said.

"How did you feel when he noticed?" the doctor asked.

Hannah pursed her lips. "Annoyed."

I looked at her sharply, but I didn't say anything.

The doctor didn't look at all surprised. "Why annoyed?"

"Because I just wanted to get it over with. I figured, once we'd done it—had sex, I mean—I wouldn't have to worry anymore. Worry that Wes might have a heart attack, worry about feeling strange…"

Kathy leaned forward. "Why would you feel strange?"

Hannah shrugged. "I don't know. It's been a while."

"Have you ever been sexually abused or traumatized, Hannah?"

"No." Hannah's face flushed.

"Those guards didn't do anything to you while they had you locked up in that condo?"

"No."

Kathy sighed. "Frankly, I find that hard to believe. I know Dr. Fisher examined you, and I know there were no signs of rape or sexual trauma. That being said, I have some concerns."

Hannah smiled at Kathy, but it was not her nice smile. "Now you sound like my sister. And Wesley, for that matter."

"Your sister and your boyfriend are concerned about you for a reason, Hannah. So is Dr. Fisher. In my experience, that sort of concern usually has a source." She paused and tilted her chin, her focus directly on Hannah. "Would you like to see me privately? We don't have to talk about this today."

I reached out and patted her knee. "Or I can leave, if you want to be alone."

Hannah sighed and put her hand over mine. "I want you to stay. I don't want to keep anything from you."

"Okay. But…are you? Keeping something from me?" My heart thudded in my chest.

Hannah sank into her chair. "No one raped me."

Kathy sat back, waiting. I held my breath.

"But one of the guards, uh, bothered me, for lack of a better word."

"Bothered you, how?" Kathy asked.

Hannah groaned. "It sounds so stupid—Wesley was shot and in a coma, and I'm whining because one of the guards harassed me."

"Harassed you while he had you captive, and he was armed, and they drugged you, and you had no means of escape. Doesn't sound like whining to me—and trust me, I *know* whining." Kathy clasped her hands together. "How did this guard harass you?"

Hannah looked from me to the doctor, and then her eyes fluttered closed, as if she didn't want to face us. "He said things to me. At first, it was that I was pretty, and then it was things about my body. Then he got more creative."

A hot ball of rage unfurled inside me. I clenched my hands into fists.

"And then?" Kathy asked.

Hannah's eyes snapped open. "And then he tried to assault me one night, but one of the other guards found him and pulled him off."

"Why did the other guard stop him?" Kathy asked.

"The guard who pulled him off was the one in charge—I think his name was Derek. He said that they were under strict instructions not to sexually assault me, and that he wasn't going to tolerate that behavior. Derek threatened to shoot the other guard if he tried it again."

Kathy pursed her lips. "But did he try it again?"

"Not exactly." Hannah went quiet for a moment and busied herself with examining her nails.

I waited, still clenching my fists, until she went on.

"He still said things to me whenever he could—nasty things. When they beat me, he always volunteered to be the one to do it." She winced. "And one night, I woke up, and he was jerking off in my face."

"I am going to kill that fucker," I said.

"He's already dead. Gabe shot him." Hannah's voice was flat.

"*Motherfucker!*" I slammed my hands against the chair.

Hannah looked at me, her eyes pleading. "Please don't get so upset. Honestly? It was disgusting, but he didn't *hurt* me."

"If it didn't hurt you, why do you think you're having a hard time connecting with Wes sexually?" Kathy asked. There was no judgment in her voice—she sounded very much the clinician, trying to understand the symptoms.

Hannah ran a hand through her hair. "The guard made me very paranoid while I was there. Even after Derek threatened him, he was always watching me. I wasn't ever sure if he'd try to cross the line again, and it made it almost impossible for me to sleep. So even though I was already in a bad situation—kidnapped, knocked around, starving—it was that extra level of stress. I just couldn't deal with it. I could deal with everything else, but I didn't want to be raped. I was worried what that would do to me—I was worried that if that happened, I'd never be the same. I wanted to be ready to fight."

"What did you do the night he was in your room? When you woke up?" Kathy asked.

"I would've bit him, but he was armed." Hannah shrugged, her lip curling in disgust. "So instead, he finished, called me a dirty, cock-teasing cunt, and left."

"Still killing him, even though he's already dead," I said. "And I wish you would've bit him."

Hannah sighed. "I wish I'd bitten him, too."

* * *

HANNAH

"You're *sure* he's dead?" Wes asked. After the appointment, he'd insisted we grab coffee and sit in a nearby park for a minute. He'd menaced Brian into standing out of earshot, and he wouldn't listen when I complained I needed to get to work.

"I was in the car when Gabe shot him. All the guards who were in the car died." I didn't look at Wesley. I watched the squirrels instead.

"I'm glad," Wes said, "but I'm also sort of not glad."

I sighed because I knew what he was saying. Wes wanted to snap the guy's neck.

"Why didn't you tell me?" he asked. "I hope I don't sound mad—I'm not. I mean, I am, but not at you."

"I didn't want to think about it. It happened, and I just wanted to keep it in the past, where it belongs."

"What do you think about what Dr. McGovern—Kathy—suggested?" he asked.

"The EMDR treatment? I don't know." I wrinkled my nose. "It sounds all weird and new-agey, not very scientific."

"Babe. You drink green smoothies every day, eat tofu, and love yoga. Isn't this sort of in your wheelhouse?" His tone was teasing as he reached over and put his big hand over mine.

"I'll think about it, okay?"

The doctor had suggested a course of EMDR, which stood for Eye Movement Desensitization and Reprocessing. I had a handout about it in my tote. The treatment supposedly worked miracles on single-trauma victims, which Kathy told me I was. Instead of prolonged talk therapy, EMDR focused on eye movements.

"*Eye* movements?" I'd asked Kathy. The treatment sounded suspiciously easy.

"Read the handout," she'd said, "and trust me. I'm licensed to administer EMDR, and it's the most promising thing I've come across in thirty years of practice. *And* you don't have to talk about your feelings, at least not for a whole hour. You would need to come in for several visits, but we'd be able to deal with your issues quickly."

That sounded encouraging—enough so I'd agreed to read the handout.

"Babe?" Wes asked, breaking my reverie.

"It could be worth a shot." I finally looked at him. "What about your homework? How do you feel about it?"

Wes frowned. "Not great."

Kathy had suggested that Wes see her separately because she felt he was holding back.

"But you're going to do what she asked, right?"

He nodded. "Yeah, I am. She seemed to know what she was talking about."

I squeezed his hand. "I'll read more about the eye therapy, okay?"

He smiled, always a good sport for me. "Okay."

I got up and pulled him toward the car. "Let's get to Paragon. We need to find out what's going on with Li Na."

I wanted to ask him about what he'd said—about living with me for safety purposes only. Did he *mean* that? Was he going to buy a new house, move out, and then we'd just…go back to dating? I couldn't imagine going to bed every night without his big, warm body next to me.

He'd been spoiling me, and I worried I'd be ruined without him.

Insecurity was a foreign feeling for me, and I hated it. *But rejection's probably worse,* I reasoned. So I kept my mouth shut, biting back the questions that were eating at me.

There was a ton of traffic on the freeway, and I bounced my knee, anxious to get to the office. My phone buzzed with a call from Fiona. "Are you okay?" I asked, not bothering to say hello.

Fiona laughed, but it sounded brittle. "Not really. Li Na Zhao sent me an email today—she wants to know where I stand on the sale of my company."

"Did she threaten you?"

Wes turned to look at me sharply.

"Not specifically," Fiona said. "But she only gave me a week to give her an answer—she said she was out of patience."

I sucked in a breath. Li Na and her ever-loving lack of patience. "What are you going to do?"

"I don't know. I scheduled a meeting with my board for tomorrow morning. I don't know what to tell them, because I don't know what to think. What will she do if I say no? After what she's already done…" Fiona started to cry, and I clenched the phone.

"I'm going to see Lauren right now. We're having a meeting about Li Na—she's been trying to hack into our system again. I'll call you afterward. We need to do something—we're in this together."

"O-okay." Fiona took a deep breath. "Can we meet up later? I really feel like I need a friend."

"Of course. You want to go to a class?"

"Only if we can get a drink afterward—and I don't mean a coconut water."

"Sounds good to me," I agreed.

"Text me later—I'll sign us up at Praise for the class tonight. And Hannah?"

"Yes?"

"Thank you."

I clutched the phone, wishing I could make things better for my friend. "Don't thank me yet."

Chapter 15

HANNAH

Lauren didn't bother to sit at our meeting; she paced the length of her office as I, Wes, Gabe, Dave, Leo, and Ash watched.

Levi was at Protocol with Ellis, making sure that Betts Security remained on high alert.

Lauren raked a hand through her hair and looked at Leo. "Explain to me again exactly what Li Na was doing in our system."

Leo took his glasses off and cleaned them while he talked. "It's like she's pinging us—going into our system and banging into our firewall. She keeps getting bounced back. It's a pretty common form of phishing. Hackers try it on a daily basis to see if there's some sort of change in their target's interface—some sort of new instability they can capitalize on."

"But why the hell is she trying to hack you again when she's already seen everything?" Gabe asked Lauren.

My sister stopped pacing and stared out the windows. "I don't know. Maybe she wants to get in again to see if we've made any improvements..."

Gabe tapped his fingers against the table, lost in thought. "Or see if you're developing anything new."

"Yeah." Lauren turned to him. "I think that could be it."

I pushed my anger and anxiety to the side for a moment to appreciate something: my sister and Gabe really were perfect for each other. In the not-too-distant past, Lauren had operated completely solo, neither seeking the opinions of others nor tolerating them. She and Gabe needed to pick a wedding date, for the love of God. I couldn't plan the wedding of the decade with Li Na hacking us and murdering our friends.

This is it. I'm DONE.

"Have we ever hacked *her*?" I asked Leo.

He nodded. "Dave and I have been able to get into her system, but Lauren had us back out after the closing didn't go through. We thought we were done with her."

"Can they go back into Jiàn Innovations' system?" I asked Lauren.

"Why would we do that? What do we have to gain?" she asked.

"I don't know, but Fiona Pace called me on our way in. Li Na gave her a week to give her an answer about selling the company."

Gabe cursed, and Lauren wrapped her arms around herself.

"I'm seeing Fiona later," I said. "I feel like we need to help. We need to do something."

"What do you want to do?" Gabe asked Lauren.

"I know what *I* want to do." I jumped up before Lauren could respond. "I want to take this bitch down, once and for all!"

Gabe grinned. "You are *so* my favorite sister-in-law."

But Lauren didn't look happy. "Hannah, I'm not sure what you have in mind."

I crossed my arms. "I don't think we've ever even talked about going after Li Na before. We've just been reacting to whatever she's throwing at us, and I'm done with that."

"You want to send me to Shenzhen to take care of her?" Wes asked, perking up.

I put my hand on my hip. "No. As in absolutely not."

"Then what?" Ash asked. "I'm not opposed to sending a team to take Li Na out—quite frankly, I think it's time. But if you have some other ideas, I'm open to hearing them."

"I've been thinking about what Gabe said. About 'face,'" I said. "I have some ideas about what to do."

"What's 'face'?" Ash asked.

"It's is a Chinese sociological concept—it's your social rank in Chinese business," I explained. "Gabe thinks it's the driving force behind Li Na's push to illegally acquire new technology. He thinks she wants to build her reputation, which in essence is her standing in the business community."

"She doesn't just care about the money," Gabe told Ash. "Li Na wants to be recognized and esteemed in her country. She's made big promises about what she's going to do for the technology industry in Shenzhen, but she's lost her chance at Paragon—twice—and failed to deliver. She's looking for a big hit."

"Paragon got away, so now she's after Protocol," I said. "She's skipping over kidnapping and blackmail, going straight to murder. She needs to close this deal fast—she must have some sort of clock ticking, something hanging over her head that's making her desperate."

"And she's back to trying to hack Paragon to see if there are any fresh ideas she can steal," Wesley added.

I stared out the windows, at the acres of neatly manicured grounds surrounding the building. "We need to make sure there's something sparkly in there so she goes for it."

"What?" Lauren asked.

I turned to my sister. "If she's looking for new technology to steal, let's give her something good."

She shook her head. "I'm not following you."

"What she cares about is her public appearance—right? She wants everyone in Shenzhen to worship her. So…what if we let her steal something from us and run with it?"

Lauren looked as if she might put her hand on my forehead to check for a fever.

"We can let her into our system and plant specs and production details about a new product we're about to launch. She can steal it, tell everyone she's about to launch some hot new technology, and then..."

"I'm still not completely following you." Lauren frowned.

"And then she'll realize that even though it's sparkly and you created it, it doesn't work. And she can fail in public."

For the first time today, I smiled.

"But we still have to deal with Fiona and Protocol Therapeutics." I turned my attention to Dave and Leo. "Last week, before she tried to hack us again, Li Na tried to insert code into Paragon's system, right?"

Dave nodded. "Yeah. It was a very sophisticated type of virus that would target certain types of files, manipulating them. We killed it before it got through, but Leo and I replicated it and played with it. The code can subtly deconstruct files, disturbing production. It can be a mess to unravel."

I snapped my fingers, then pointed to Dave. "*That* is what I'm talking about. We need to boomerang that code and disrupt Li Na's system."

Dave stroked his patchy beard, looking confused. "Huh?"

"So that even if Fiona sells to Li Na, the antibody therapy is compromised. But not until *after* she gets it and gets ready to launch. Because we need to humiliate her in public. Because *that* is what that bitch fears most, and I am going to serve it up to her in a one-two punch!"

I turned around, beaming at everyone, thrumming with adrenaline.

Gabe and Lauren looked at each other. Wes cocked his head, examining me.

"You don't get it, do you?" I asked, deflating.

Lauren opened her mouth and then closed it. Gabe scratched his head.

"I think we need to process," Wes said. "That's all."

I stood and grabbed my tote. "Fine—process. I'm meeting Fiona. I'll see you all at home. Dave, Leo? Can you keep working on that code for me? These guys will come around."

I glared at each of them individually before I left. They *better*.

* * *

"Ellis is staying in the room during class?" I asked as I assembled my mat and towel next to Fiona's. Brian had at least agreed to wait in the lobby, even if he was stalking around and scowling.

Fiona sighed. "He doesn't talk much, and he also doesn't take no for an answer." She brushed the bangs from her face and inspected Ellis, who stood at rigid attention at the wall of the studio. "He's kind of intimidating, don't you think?"

"He has a heart of gold underneath the glower. He's just very serious."

I studied Ellis. He wore a long-sleeve shirt, jeans, and heavy boots. The temperature in the room would soon rise above one hundred degrees, and there would be lots of bodies in the studio, sweating profusely. "He might die if he keeps all those clothes on."

"When I mentioned it, he said he was fine."

"Let me talk to him."

I got up and approached Wes's brother. "Hey."

His blue eyes, so much like Wes's, flicked to mine. "Hey."

"You're going to get too hot with those jeans on," I told him.

A ghost of a smile lit up his face. "So I've been told."

"Do you have to stay in here, against the wall? It's kind of weird."

He looked at Fiona. "I am not letting her out of my sight for a second, but thank you."

"How's she doing?" I kept my voice low.

He just shook his head.

"If you feel dizzy, go wait outside. I'm not going to let anything happen to her."

Ellis looked unimpressed as he inspected my pink tank top and pink-and-white camouflage capris tights. "I think I can handle it."

I gave him a dirty look that I didn't mean in any way, shape, or form. I loved Wes's brother—he'd been kind to me from the first moment I met him, even though Wes was seriously injured while protecting me. "Fine," I huffed, heading back to my mat.

Ellis didn't budge.

Fiona eyed him. "He's stubborn."

"Stubborn's probably good." I sighed. "Stubborn will protect you."

I wanted to talk more, but the instructor came in, and the room fell silent. Talking during yoga was a no-no, as were cell phones. Fiona and I followed instructions, gamely moving through the poses as the room grew hotter. We did sun salutations, upward-facing dogs, downward-facing dogs, forward folds, and halfway lifts.

By the time we'd warmed up and gotten to Warrior One, sweat poured off me.

I glanced at Fiona. Not only was she sweating, tears were coursing down her face.

"Are you all right?" I whispered.

"Yes." She quickly wiped her eyes.

Throughout the rest of the class, tears streamed down her face. I wasn't the only one to notice—the instructor came over, a kind, insanely fit woman in her fifties who looked like she could bench press me. The teacher whispered, "Are you okay?"

Fiona nodded. "I just lost my husband."

"The tears are a release—as you release the physical tension, you release the emotional tension." The instructor patted Fiona on the shoulder. "Good work."

I thought I heard Ellis snort from his post on the wall.

I ignored him and prayed Fiona did, too.

After class ended, I cleaned my mat and checked on Fiona.

"That was intense. I still need a drink." She looked down at herself. Her shirt was drenched and sticking to her skin. "I guess I need to shower?"

"There's a dive bar down the street," I offered. "If we put our sweatshirts on and sit far away from everyone else, maybe no one can smell us."

Fiona smiled. It was the first smile I'd seen from her in a long time. "Then let's go, but quick. I need to get home to Katie and Quinn—I was at the office before this. It's the longest I've been gone."

"Of course."

Ellis followed us out, and I noticed there was a sheen of sweat on his forehead. "What did you think of the class?"

He rolled his eyes, which told me plenty.

Ellis and Brian didn't sit with us at the table we selected in the dark bar—they stood near the door, alert and watching the few patrons' every move.

"How are the girls doing?" I asked.

Fiona considered her vodka and soda. "They love having my mom at the house. They asked her to move in with us."

"Aw, that's sweet."

"Except that she said yes, and I haven't lived with my mom since I was eighteen." Fiona poked the straw into her glass, swirling the ice around. "It'll be nice, I guess. To have someone home. Jim usually got out of work before me…"

I reached over and squeezed her hand. "How're you holding up?"

She shook her head. "I'm crying at yoga. I cried at my board meeting. I cry in the shower."

"It's normal, if that makes you feel any better." From my experience, I knew it wouldn't.

"My other issue is that Li Na is pressing me to sell my company. And after what she did, I'm too afraid to say no. If anything ever happened to my girls…" She shuddered. "I don't want to sell her this technology because it has so much promise. It can help so many people. But I can't help being selfish—after what happened to Jim, I'm too afraid. I don't want to say no to her."

I leaned forward. "Then don't."

"I'm sorry?"

"I've been thinking about it. I have some insight into what Li Na wants, and I've started coming up with a plan."

Fiona took a large gulp of her drink. "*You* have?"

I tried not to take offense at her tone. "I know my sister's the brilliant one, but I have my own ideas—"

"That's not what I meant. I've worked with you. I know that you're brilliant in your own right. But I *also* know that you have a big heart, and I've never seen you be unkind, even to people who might deserve it."

"Li Na exists on a whole new level of deserving. I'm more than ready to be unkind. So here's what I'm thinking…"

* * *

WES

I'd never been so glad to see a steak in my life. I popped another bite of filet into my mouth and moaned. "This is delicious."

Gabe laughed. "I have to sneak out here at least once a week—don't tell Lauren. I'm pretty sure the soy's going to kill me."

I clinked my glass against his. "Amen. If I never see another piece of bean curd…"

"You're dating the tofu queen," he reminded me. "Good luck."

Gabe had kept his word about organizing a men-only steakhouse dinner. Ash, Gabe, and I had met Levi after we left Paragon. The trendy restaurant was packed on a Friday night. We were seated in a large booth, finishing our second round of drinks.

"I'm keeping a list of things to tell Lauren." Levi eyed Gabe over his bourbon. "I'm telling her about you cheating on her with steak. She's too good for you, and she should know it."

"Don't start." Gabe glowered at his older brother. "Or I'll tell Bethany how much you've been checking in with her bodyguard."

"What's this?" Ash leaned forward, eyes sparkling. "He's stalking Lauren's hot lawyer again?"

Gabe grinned. "He calls her bodyguard twice a day. I heard him ask if Bethany had *mentioned* him."

Ash and Gabe howled with laughter as Levi fumed.

Being with the brothers reminded me of Ellis. I'd asked him to join us, but he refused to take time off. I shot him a quick text as Levi argued with Gabe and Ash.

How's it going with Fiona?

No threats, no suspicious people.

I meant, how's she doing?

She cries a lot.

My brother didn't do emotions. He never cried, even when our parents died.

Are you…being nice to her?

Do you really think I'm that much of a dick?

No, I typed quickly. *Sort of,* I thought.

"Not to interrupt, but are you going to make it official with my future sister-in-law?" Gabe asked.

I coughed, almost choking on the steak. "There's an awful lot of gossip happening at this table. I'm feeling emasculated—can't we talk about the game?"

"We could." Gabe cut another piece of steak. "Or we could talk about work, instead…"

Everyone booed. We were still mulling Hannah's somewhat out-there idea about trapping Li Na.

"How about another round instead?" Gabe suggested.

This time, we met him with cheers.

* * *

I wasn't drunk, but I wasn't exactly sober when I got into bed later. Hannah slept soundly, rolled over on her side. She didn't move when I climbed in next to her.

I leaned closer, careful not to wake her as I inhaled the heady mix of her scent—some sort of hippie-ish essential oil and her own smell, clean and healthy. She smelled like sunlight.

I thought about what she'd told the shrink. About what that guard had done to her.

I cringed, wishing I'd been able to be there for her, to help. I also wished that I'd been the one to kill the bastard. That was a terrible wish, I knew, but he'd hurt her…terrorized her, preying on her when she was at her most vulnerable.

Sonofabitch.

But he was gone, and I had to let it go. Now I needed to support Hannah as she led the charge against Li Na. I'd never seen her pissed like this before. In addition to the fact that it was sort of hot, I loved watching her mind work.

That wasn't all that I loved.

No matter what happened, I had to keep her safe. Because if Li Na came after us again?

This time, I'd be ready.

Chapter 16

FIONA

I watched Katie and Quinn as they slept. Their faces were relaxed, a far cry from how they'd looked in the terrible days since their dad died. My poor girls. I took another step into the semidarkness of their room, making sure that each of their chests was rising and falling.

When they were babies, Jim and I took turns checking on them. We were both paranoid—a fact I relied on and relished. We used to joke that the kids never slept through the night because we were always poking and prodding them, making sure they were breathing okay.

I clutched my chest as I watched the girls sleep peacefully now. *Oh, Jim…*

I heard a noise behind me and whirled.

"It's just me," Ellis said.

It was the most he'd said since he'd been assigned to protect me.

"I was just checking on them." I kept my voice low.

"I get it."

I stepped out of the girls' room and headed to the kitchen, Ellis close on my heels. At first, I'd been unnerved by his constant, silent presence. But I'd gotten used to him. It felt safer having his six-foot-four, two-hundred-and-something pounds of pure muscle nearby.

I went to the fridge and stared inside, wondering if he'd judge me for having a glass of wine. I poured one anyway. "Would you like a drink?" I asked.

"No, thank you." He crossed his arms and leaned against the wall.

I watched as his eyes flicked methodically around the room, then out the window to the driveway. There were three other armed guards outside, but I'd noticed Ellis still periodically did a perimeter scan.

My thoughts wandered over the day, pausing for a moment on the embarrassment of crying during yoga. Jesus. *I'm such a mess.* I allowed myself a shudder, then moved on. Missing my husband wasn't a weakness—it was human to mourn him, and I refused to punish myself for it. I'd been suffering enough.

I thought back on the conversation I'd had with Hannah after class. What she'd proposed had surprised me, and my immediate gut reaction was a hard no. License my technology to the woman who'd killed my husband? And then reverse-engineer a hack to ruin it? Hannah was asking me to play with fire, a fire that could consume the rest of what remained of my family.

I couldn't take that risk. But was it riskier to do nothing and leave my family vulnerable?

"I'm sorry," Ellis said, interrupting my train of thought, "but what are you thinking about?"

"What?" I startled, having forgotten he was standing there. He'd never asked me a question before.

"The look on your face... Can I help?"

I sighed. I was leaking so much that even my monosyllabic bodyguard had noticed. "I'm just trying to figure something out, and I don't know what the answer is. Normally, that's not a problem for me." Making good decisions had always been easy for me, a point of pride. But for the moment, I felt lost.

"If you need to talk about it, you can. I might not be able to help, but I can at least listen."

"Thank you." I swirled my wine around, wondering if he'd find me even more ridiculous if I spoke further.

I took another sip of Fumé blanc for courage. "Hannah had an idea about how to deal with Li Na Zhao. She suggested that I let Protocol license the antibody therapy to her, then compromise the technology, so it doesn't perform. So it malfunctions." It seemed dangerous to say it out loud.

Ellis nodded, waiting for me to continue.

"I think it's a good idea—maybe the only shot I have for a preemptive strike. I don't know if I want to do it, but only because I'm afraid Li Na will come after us. That she'll…" I couldn't say it aloud. I thought of Katie and Quinn sleeping safely in their room, and I felt sick.

"I can't tell you what to do with your business, but I'll protect you and the girls. No matter what. I won't let anyone hurt you. You don't have to include your fear as a factor."

I looked at his massive form, touched. "I know you're very good at your job, but can you actually promise that?"

"It's the only thing I can promise."

"Thank you." I didn't know if his assurance was enough, but it was something.

Ellis nodded again, and I sensed the conversation was over.

"Well, good night." I paused at the door. "Do you *sleep*?"

He'd been with me for over a week, and he'd barely taken time off. I'd been so consumed with grief and anxiety, I hadn't even wondered if he was taking care of himself.

"Less than I talk."

I might've imagined it, but I thought he smiled. At least a little.

* * *

HANNAH

I scowled at Dr. Kathy, the therapist, as I sat on the couch. She arranged a long box at eye level in front of me. It had a row of small lightbulbs running across it horizontally.

"What *is* that thing?"

She tucked a corkscrew curl behind her ear and plugged the box in. "It's a light box. I'm going to use it to help alleviate your negative thoughts."

I crossed my legs and bounced my knee nervously. "I don't think I have any negative thoughts."

Kathy appeared to ignore me as she gathered her file and sat in a nearby chair. Then she asked, "So what was that panic attack all about?"

I sighed. "I was upset about Jim's murder. Once you add that event on top of all the other crazy that's been going on in my life, it's clear why I had anxiety. But I'm fine. It hasn't happened again."

"Have you experienced any other symptoms?" she asked.

"No. I mean, I'm a little anxious in general, but that seems normal to me."

"Have you and Wesley had sex yet?"

I grimaced. "No."

"Does it make you anxious to think about it?"

I picked at some invisible lint on my blouse. "Maybe a little. I just want to get it over with, but then I feel guilty for feeling that way."

Kathy pointed her finger at me. "That feeling—that guilt—is what we're going to eradicate with EMDR. That guilt is a negative thought, a consequence of the trauma you experienced. If you relax and try this for me, I promise you won't be disappointed. And remember, you're doing this for you *and* for Wesley."

"That's manipulative—you know I'd do anything for Wes."

She smiled brightly. "I know, but I'm a therapist. I have to work with the skills I've got! So, are you ready?"

I swallowed over a sudden lump in my throat.

Kathy reached over and grabbed my hand. "It's not that difficult, I swear. It's better than living this way."

"Okay."

"EMDR can be done several ways. The one I have experience with is using this box," she tapped the light box, "and it's proven very effective."

I scowled at the box, unconvinced.

Kathy sat back against her chair. "I want you to go back to that image you shared with me—when you woke up and the guard was standing over you, masturbating."

I shivered.

"How did that make you feel?"

"I felt vulnerable…helpless. I felt afraid, which *really* pissed me off."

"And what thoughts were you having the night you had the panic attack?"

"I was thinking about my friend's husband who was killed, how sad my friend and her daughters were. And then I kept thinking about Wes, when he got shot and when he was hooked up to all those machines at the hospital." I shivered. "And my parents, I thought about when I saw my mom after she died…"

"And how did those thoughts make you feel?"

"Panicked, obviously." I laughed, but it sounded brittle, like I might break. "Hopeless. Helpless. Angry."

"Good job." Kathy motioned toward the box. "Now take a deep breath and get ready. I want you to watch the lights. Bring that memory back up—the guard standing over you. How did that make you feel?"

I watched the tiny lights blink across the box as I recounted the memory. "I felt powerless—disgusted with myself because I felt so weak."

The light sequence finished, and I blinked.

"Excellent," Kathy said.

I wrinkled my nose. She had a weird concept of "excellent."

She leaned forward. "Take a deep breath. Let's try this again…"

* * *

"Do you think it worked?" Lauren asked. I'd brought lunch to Paragon, but she was only pushing her grilled salmon around inside its reusable container.

"I don't know." I still hadn't told Lauren the full extent of what had happened with the guard who'd assaulted me—I didn't want to burden her with any more guilt. But I'd explained that the therapist was treating me with EMDR for my anxiety.

"How does the light impact you, exactly?" Lauren's scientific brain craved details.

I chewed my quinoa thoughtfully, trying to remember exactly what Kathy had said. "At first she had me think of something that was bothering me—a negative thought that was causing me anxiety—and then she asked me how the thought made me feel."

"I need an example," Lauren said. "I can't picture this."

"My negative thought was that when the guards had me, I felt helpless. I felt powerless, and that's seriously stressful for me. So the other night, when I had a panic attack and my body went out of control, I felt powerless all over again, and it was this self-fulfilling episode of…crap, for lack of a better word. Mental crap that incapacitated me."

Lauren's shoulders slumped.

"I'm not telling you this if you're going to get upset."

She frowned. "Fine. Tell me how the therapy works."

"The doctor had me say my negative thought out loud, and she ran the light box at the same time. The idea behind is that you activate the old memory to short-term memory at the same time your eyes track the light. Supposedly the memory becomes blurred, and the bad memory loses some of its power." I wrinkled my nose, unsure if I'd explained it right. "Does that make sense?"

"Absolutely." Lauren's eyes lit up—science excited her. "The treatment disrupts the negative thought process. The sequencing allows the brain to make new connections while the negative thought is present. It's pretty brilliant in its simplicity." Satisfied, she finally took a bite of her lunch.

I laughed.

"What?"

"I'm glad it makes sense to you. I thought my doctor was crazy when she sat me in front of a lightbox, but if you think there's a valid scientific reason for it, that's good enough for me."

"Do you feel better?"

"I don't know. I think so? My anxiety has been..." *Situational.* I refused to say it out loud. Wesley and I still hadn't had sex, and *that* was starting to cause me anxiety. "Minimal."

Lauren didn't look fooled. "Go to the follow-up appointments."

"Yes, ma'am. I already put them in my calendar. But enough about that—where are we with my proposed plan for Li Na?"

Lauren hadn't mentioned it, and I'd been dying to know her thoughts.

She smiled, a gleam lighting up her eyes. "I had an idea."

"For...?"

The smile widened into a grin. "A prototype we can upload to Paragon's server—something to tempt Li Na with. I've been secretly working on this technology for months, and it's shiny and glittery and full of promise, but it doesn't work yet. It has a flaw."

I leaned forward. "Is the flaw so tiny only my brilliant CEO-scientist sister would be able to notice it?"

"That's right." Lauren looked pleased with herself. "Li Na's a wannabe—she would never flag this design defect until it's too late. At least, I think she wouldn't. I still need to work on how to present the specs, but the thoughts have been coming fast and fierce."

I clapped my hands together. "Yes! I want to hear all the details." My phone buzzed, and I glanced at it—a text from Fiona.

I've decided to go ahead with the agreement with Jiàn...and the plan.

Excellent. I'm in a meeting. Call you later to talk.

I did a double fist-pump. "This is *totally* turning into my day."

"What was that?" Lauren asked.

"Fiona wants to go ahead with what we discussed. She wants to exclusively license her technology to Li Na, and then have Dave and Leo infect it with the code they reverse-engineered."

My sister's eyebrow arched. "Li Na's going to go ballistic with all this new technology. My new prototype actually dovetails with Fiona's—she's not going to be able to resist either one of them. She's going to be excited. You know what this means, don't you?"

"We're getting rid of Li Na once and for all? We might actually make her *cry*?" The idea made me giddy.

"No. It means that if we don't take her down for good this time, we're screwed." She raised her gaze to meet mine. "All of us."

I swallowed over a sudden lump in my throat. "Well, we know what we're doing." I hoped. "And the time is now—after killing Jim, and everything else that she's done, we have to stop her. We can't keep living like this."

Lauren nodded. "I know. It's crazy that we all have round-the-clock security. And trust me, I want to make her pay for what she's done."

"We all do." I went quiet for a second, wondering how to broach the next topic. "I actually had another idea."

"I'm listening."

"What if we—and I should preface this by saying that not only have I not thought this all the way through, you aren't going to approve, but—what if we hire someone at Jiàn Innovations to work for us? It would be helpful if we had someone on the inside to keep us updated so we're not sitting over here, holding our collective breath while we wait to find out if and when Li Na's plans are going to implode."

"How do you propose we do that?"

I shrugged. "Li Na had Clive Warren working for her."

Clive Warren had been a board member at Paragon, but he'd been lured to the dark side and had worked with Li Na to try to steal the company from my sister.

Unfortunately for Clive, the only place his allegiance had got him was jail, where he was murdered.

Lauren looked unconvinced. "Li Na threatened Clive Warren—that was the only reason he worked for her. That, and because she probably made him all sorts of wild promises in the beginning."

I shrugged again.

"Hannah! We are not getting involved in that sort of criminal activity!"

"But we need someone to let us know if Li Na's working on the specs you plant and what the status is with the Protocol technology. We need an informant. I'm not suggesting we *stab* them."

Lauren crossed her arms. "Then what are you suggesting?"

I took a deep breath. "We could always just threaten them, a little…"

She shook her head. "I'm willing to entertain all possibilities, but this is moving in a questionable direction awfully fast. Listen, it's Friday. I want you to take the weekend off."

"Since when did we take weekends off?"

Lauren planted her hands on her hips. "*You* take weekends off when I order you to—last time I checked, I'm still your boss. You're going full throttle, but you just got back on your feet. I want you to take a couple of days."

I sprang out of my chair. "You're saying that as my big sister, not as my boss, and we both know it."

"That may be true"—her face softened—"but that doesn't mean I'm taking it back."

"Fine. But we need to move on this. I'm done waiting for Li Na to terrorize us again."

Lauren sighed. "I want you to think this whole thing through and then come back on Monday morning with a clear line."

"What kind of line?"

Lauren's blue eyes, so much like my own, bore into me. "The kind you aren't willing to cross. We'll go from there. Now, go away with Wesley and have fun. Be young. Be carefree."

At the mention of Wes, I frowned, playing with the pages of my notebook.

My sister, who missed nothing, frowned back. "What's the matter?"

"It's about Wes. He said he was buying a new house—he's letting Ellis have the old one."

"Okay. So why do you look like you might cry?"

"Because what if he buys a new house?"

Lauren twisted a lock of hair, looking stymied. "Then he'll…have a new house?"

"And what? I'll still be with you guys? I'll buy my own house?"

"You can stay with us forever," Lauren soothed, clearly misunderstanding me. She thought I was afraid of being alone.

"I don't want to stay with you forever, and I don't want to buy my own house." I bit my lip.

"So, what *do* you want?"

"I want to be with Wes. I don't want to just be young and carefree and have a fun weekend or only be living with him because it's safer that way."

Lauren's face softened. "I'm glad you're bringing this up, because I want to talk to you. But I don't want you to get mad at me."

"Okay…"

"Bear with me, it's a little circuitous."

I laughed. "Lauren, I'm used to the crazy-brilliant way you think."

She sighed. "Li Na's responsible for a lot. She hurt you, and she hurt me, and she hurt Wes. And Jim… She's done terrible things."

"I'm aware of them," I said, still wary.

"I just don't want you to…*react* to her."

"I had a panic attack the other night, and I'm considering blackmailing one of her employees into working for us, remember? I think I've already failed."

"You didn't fail, but I'm worried. Ugh, I don't know how to say this."

"So, it's personal—whatever it is you need to say."

Personal was difficult for Lauren, even with me.

She bit her lip.

"Just spit it out."

"I think it's nice that you have Wesley, especially during this difficult time. It's great."

I arched an eyebrow. "But?"

"But, I don't…I don't want you to feel like you *have* to be so serious with him, just because he got shot for you."

I almost fell out of my chair. "You think that's why I'm with him? Because he took a bullet for me and almost died?"

"No. But it would certainly be understandable."

I shook my head. "That's not why we're together."

Lauren looked miserable. "But you haven't exactly ever been serious about a guy before. This all seems very sudden. You went from casually dating to both being traumatized, and now you're about to lose it because he's buying a new house?"

I scoffed. "I've never been serious about a guy before because I hadn't met the right one. *Wesley* is the right one." Now that I said it out loud, I knew it was true.

"I care about Wes, too, but I don't want you to make him a promise because you feel like you *should*."

I stood to go. "I'm not—I wouldn't hurt him like that. And yes, I think I *will* take the weekend off. Think about what I said about Li Na's employee. It's about time you started taking me seriously."

Chapter 17

WES

"I can't do that again."

I looked up at Ashley, miserable.

She squatted down near me and tucked a dreadlock behind her ear. "You've been out of your wheelchair for over a week. Over a whole week *and you didn't even tell me. And you didn't have permission.* So now that you have permission, and you've been semi back at the office and out to dinner and doing God only knows what else, you bet your sweet ass that you can do it again."

She sprang back up. "Now *move.*"

I grabbed the resistance bands and stood up. "If I die, it's on your conscience."

She arched an eyebrow at me. "I'll blame *you*. At your *gravesite*. Now like I said, get moving!"

I cursed, adjusted the bands, and got moving.

Later, as the driver took me to my therapy appointment, my cell phone rang. My arms were so sore, I could barely lift the phone to my ear.

"I need you to get Hannah out of here for the weekend," Lauren said by way of a greeting. "She's been working too much, and with everything that's happened, I think she needs a break."

"Are you sure she'll be okay with that?"

Lauren sighed. "I told her to stay out of the office until Monday—the only way she'll unplug is if you keep her busy."

"I'll do what I can."

"I really appreciate it. I know I'm interfering."

I chuckled. "What else is new?"

"Wes, I need to say something. I'm sorry about what I said, about the couples' therapy."

She caught me by surprise. "Oh?"

"I didn't mean to minimize your relationship with Hannah. I know how much she cares for you. It's serious."

Lauren struggled to get the words out—talking about personal stuff was not her style.

"She does? It is?" I asked.

I couldn't help it—the words got out before I could play it cool.

"She really does. Do you…are you…is it…reciprocal?"

Big sister, ever protective, was looking out for Hannah.

Luckily, Lauren and I were on the same team. "Yes, it is. Completely."

She sighed in relief. "Okay, good. *Great.*"

We hung up, and I looked out the window at the traffic, grinning. I liked Lauren's proposal, but I didn't know if Hannah would want to take a quick getaway—for a number of reasons. She wouldn't want to leave Paragon with everything that was going on. Also, she might not want the pressure of being alone with me in a sexy hotel room. I hoped that wasn't true, but it might be. I needed to give her space until she was ready.

Still, I sighed, thinking about having her all to myself for the weekend. *Especially if she feels the way I do.* My body throbbed selfishly until we pulled up in front of the doctor's office, and then all thoughts of sexy hotel rooms promptly fled, replaced by dread.

"Hannah was here earlier this morning, you know," Kathy told me as I lowered myself onto her rumpled love seat. My thighs screamed, and inwardly I cursed Ashley.

I sat uncomfortably, wishing I could flee. "Yeah, I know. How'd it go?"

The doctor adjusted her lavender glasses. "I think it went very well. She's coming back early next week to repeat the therapy, and I believe that after another few sessions, her anxiety will have significantly abated."

"That's wonderful."

"It really is. You two still haven't been intimate, correct?"

I sighed. "Correct."

"What do you think about that?"

Guess I wasn't getting around *this* topic today.

"I think…we need to wait until Hannah's ready. Her sister just called me—she wants me to take Hannah out of town for the weekend. She's been working nonstop, and Lauren wants her to take a break. But I don't know if that's too much pressure, you know—taking her away to some fancy hotel."

Kathy tilted her chin, inspecting me. "What about you? Is that too much pressure on *you*?"

"I'm ready."

The doctor watched me closely, and I groaned.

"I mean, I want to, but I don't want to." I clenched and unclenched my fists. I couldn't believe I was talking to this stranger, a middle-aged woman wearing some smock-like dress, about my nonexistent sex life. "Do we really have to talk about this?"

Kathy didn't even blink. "Do you really want to avoid talking about it and hope it just blows over?"

I scratched my head. "Is it bad if I say yes?"

"No, it's not. But you have to recognize that you won't be as prepared as you could be, and that won't be the best thing for Hannah."

I grimaced as she struck the nerve she'd been looking for. "Do *you* recognize that you're being very manipulative by putting it to me that way?"

She grinned at me. "Yes, I do. And for the record, I'd just like to say how perfect I think you and Hannah are for each other."

"Okay…"

Kathy gently smiled. "I know it's manipulative of me to tell you to consider Hannah—still, you have to consider her. And I know that's why you're here. You want to get better for her."

"I don't need to get better—I'm fine." I waited for her to object, but she said nothing, so after I minute I asked, "Unless you disagree?"

She watched me, not saying anything.

"Is this the part where you sit and wait for me to spill my guts and make an ass out of myself?"

She arched an eyebrow. "No, but I'm sure that'd be amusing. Please proceed."

I coughed. "I don't feel messed up. I was angry, and I'm still angry about what happened to her and to my coworkers that night. And about the fact that I couldn't protect her, that I wasn't there, that I was injured, that I'm still not better yet…"

Kathy nodded.

"Are you *agreeing* with me?" My voice came out sharper than I intended.

"No. I was just signifying that I was listening."

"Oh." I looked at my lap, unsure of what I felt or what, if anything, I should say. *Jesus, get me out of here.* Therapy might be as bad as tofu. It might be worse.

She sat there, waiting for me to continue.

"I don't like feeling helpless," I said eventually.

"Of course you don't." Kathy's voice was soothing. "You're a marine, and you've been on your own for a long time. You're not the type of person who sits back and watches others get hurt—you're the guy who protects people."

"I didn't protect her. I didn't protect the other agents."

"They shot you. They incapacitated you."

I clenched my hands into fists. "Then they took her from me…and you know what they did."

"But she's okay. She's going to be fine. And Wes, what happened to her wasn't your fault."

"You're wrong about that." I shook my head. "We were joking around. I was supposed to be guarding her, but we were in her kitchen joking around. The other guys were outside, and I never even heard what happened to them—because I *wasn't paying attention*. I was in the kitchen. I was joking around. *I wasn't paying attention*."

"Even if that's true, you aren't responsible for what happened to the other men—"

"The hell I'm not!"

"It's not any different from the service," Kathy continued. "Everyone knows what they're signing up for. The work you do is dangerous work. The men who died that night aren't any different from the other peers you've lost over the years—and you haven't told me much, but I know you've lost people."

I didn't look up. "Not only did they die that night, but Hannah got kidnapped. *That is on me*."

Kathy nodded. "Okay."

"*Now* you're agreeing with me?"

"Now I'm agreeing with you."

I shot up, then realized that the sudden movement made my legs scream in pain again. *Motherf-ing physical therapy.* "I think I'm done here."

"I can't stop you physically, or by asking you to reconsider, but I think it would be in your best interest if you sat back down. *Your* best interest. And Hannah's."

"Really? The Hannah card again?" But I flopped back down.

"I know you want to move forward. As a first step, you might want to stop beating yourself up." She motioned to my legs. "I think you've been pushing yourself too hard, too fast. I'm not sure what the rush is."

"The rush is that the woman who did all this is still out there, and she's killed another innocent person. The *rush* is that the next time someone threatens people I care about, I am not going to fuck it up."

"You were *shot*. You were *hurt*. Bad people did something terrible to you and you couldn't protect *yourself*. Don't forget about yourself!"

"That's not the point—"

"It is absolutely the point. As much as you've focused on everything you didn't do, who you couldn't save, you've only been punishing yourself, and you were wounded, Wesley. You almost *died*. You're twenty-seven, and you almost died. And you haven't even been kind enough to let yourself heal. You've been pushing hard."

"That's what I needed to do, though." I scrubbed a hand across my face. "That's the only thing that makes me feel sane."

Kathy switched gears. "So…what's your plan for being intimate with Hannah?"

"I don't know yet." I felt dizzy from her zigzagging across topics. "I want it to be special, really special."

Kathy sighed. "I think that's too much pressure."

"Why? It's been months…she went through so much…"

"You've both been through so much," she corrected me. "And as someone who is treating both of you, I think trying to make it especially special is putting too much pressure on the situation."

"What do you recommend?"

"Go away this weekend, have a glass of wine, and then have sex. Don't overthink it." She shrugged. "I don't think I'm violating patient confidentiality by telling you that Hannah is just as anxious as you are for things to get back to normal—the new normal—between you two. I think you should follow Hannah's lead in a way that makes the experience just as authentic and healing for you."

"I'll see if I can do that." *If I can figure out what the hell that means.*

She cocked her head and looked at me again. "Our time is almost up. Anything else you want to talk about?"

I was more than ready to be done, but I *did* need help with something. "Just one question." I paused for a beat. "How can I tell Hannah I hate tofu?"

Kathy almost spit her tea out. "She's a vegetarian?"

"She eats fish. But she's really pushing the tofu."

Kathy wrinkled her nose.

"She keeps making it for me. Marinated. Grilled. Infused with kimchi."

"I'm sorry to hear that."

I sighed. "Apparently, the fact that it's a vegetable-based protein is going to save the world from climate change. And of course, she likes to stress the fact that it's cruelty-free and Bambi didn't have to die for it."

"My ex-husband was vegan. I feel your pain." Kathy shuddered. "But Hannah's feelings for you appear unconditional. Go ahead and order a nice steak this weekend."

Maybe therapy wasn't as bad as a slab of rectangular bean curd.

She smiled. "Have a nice weekend. I want you to come back and see me again next week—alone *and* with Hannah. I want to hear about your progress in the bedroom."

On second thought…

* * *

Hannah slid off her blazer and looked curiously at our bed. "Baby? Why is our luggage out?"

"Because we're going to Point Reyes for the weekend."

Hannah put a hand on her hip and scowled. "Did my sister call you?"

Of course she did.

"No. I just thought it would be fun. You remember fun, don't you?"

"Ha-ha. I *invented* fun." She bit her lip. "I want to go, but there's some stuff I really need to deal with."

"Your boss gave you the weekend off. In fact, she insists."

"I knew Lauren was behind this!"

I held up my hands. "I have good ideas too, you know. I booked a sick resort for us—and get this, it's rated the 'top green' hotel in the country. They have poolside yoga. And an antioxidant smoothie bar."

Hannah's eyes lit up, and I chuckled.

"Are you teasing me?"

"A little. About the smoothie bar."

She sighed, but she was still smiling.

I captured her hand under mine, and she leaned down for a lingering kiss.

"Is that a yes?" I asked when she pulled back.

"Like I can say no to you." She went to the closet and started whipping out outfits. "It'll be nice for us to hang out. And I've heard there're some cool hiking trails down there I've been dying to check out…"

She chatted happily. I watched her examining lingerie, and as she folded it neatly, an unbidden thought popped into my head: *Does my dick still even work?*

I swallowed nervously. I had a feeling I was about to find out.

* * *

We had a driver and Brian with us for the two-hour drive, along with three additional Betts security agents in another car.

"Nothing like a weekend just for two," Hannah joked.

"They'll give us plenty of space. Right, Brian?"

Brian rolled his eyes. "We've got the entire floor at the resort rented out. We'll be there at the ready—we've got you covered."

"Great," I said under my breath. I turned my attention back to Hannah. "What's the latest at Paragon?"

"Lauren and I are working on that new…initiative." Her eyes sparkled.

"The prototype?"

"Yes, the one we discussed at the meeting—Lauren's been brainstorming plans, and she thinks she might have something ready to go soon. And Fiona's decided to go ahead and license her technology to Li Na and then use that technology we discussed."

The technology that would disrupt the antibody therapy's design from the inside out.

"When did she decide that?"

"Today. We talked a little while ago. She said Ellis promised to protect her and the girls no matter what, so she felt safe enough to go for it."

I arched an eyebrow. "Ellis made her a *promise?*"

"Yes." Hannah's eyes were wide. "It meant the world to Fiona. She said he makes her feel safe, and that even the girls have been able to sleep because they're getting used to having security around. I'll have to do something nice for him. Fiona's so crushed about Jim, it's a blessing that at least she feels safe."

"Huh." I was going to have ask my brother about all this. He must really be taking his new civilian status seriously. "What else is going on?"

Lauren had been adamant that Hannah take a few days off. There had to be something more.

Hannah played with a lock of her blonde hair. "I've proposed hiring a Jiàn Innovations employee to simultaneously work for Paragon. I need to make an offer to someone when we get back."

"Excuse me?"

Her mouth twisted. "I'm hiring one of Li Na's employees to spy for us."

"Um…are you sure that's a good idea?"

The last thing I wanted was for Hannah to get in Li Na's line of sight again. I wanted her completely under the radar, not poking the bear.

Hannah pushed her shoulders back. "I'm absolutely sure it's a good idea. We've been too passive for too long with Li Na—it's time to go on offense. I need to make sure this works so we can *ruin* her."

"Okay?" I couldn't agree with her, but the blush in her cheeks and the firm set of her jaw indicated disagreeing with her was not my best move at the moment.

"Okay." She put her hand over mine and squeezed. "Enough about all that. How was physical therapy today? And regular therapy?"

I shook my head. "I think both of those women might be trying to kill me."

Hannah giggled.

"It's not funny."

I told her more about my day until we pulled down the long drive toward Solange, the resort I'd booked, a little while later. The Spanish-tiled, sprawling building was softly lit with twinkling white lights. A massive fountain bubbled next to a large tree with low-hanging branches. The intimate, sparkling courtyard had a magical feel, making me wonder if wood nymphs or very expensive gnomes lived somewhere nearby.

Hannah sighed deeply. "Oh Wes, this is gorgeous. It's so serene—I love it."

I grinned, proud of my googling skills (and also that I'd taken Gabe's advice to book this particular resort). "It's okay."

I tried to hide my wince as I got out of the car, but, as usual, Hannah missed nothing.

"What the hell did Ashley *do* to you today?"

I shrugged, but even that hurt my muscles. "She punished me for going rogue and getting rid of the wheelchair. But it doesn't matter"—I gestured to the bellhops, who were collecting our bags—"everything's taken care of. I don't need to lift a finger."

I tried not to grimace as we climbed the steps to the entrance, but Hannah still frowned at me.

All frowning ceased as we entered the lobby, which boasted a floor-to-ceiling fireplace, gorgeous tiled floors, and more artfully arranged couches than I could process.

"This is stunning," Hannah said. "Wow."

Our suite was even better—we had our own private courtyard, complete with a plunge pool and several bottles of local wines chilling in the dedicated wine fridge.

I grabbed a bottle of Pinot and opened it. The plunge pool and what Hannah and I could do in it were already making me sweat. *Could Brian and the other guys hear us out there?*

"We did not have accommodations like this in the marines."

"This is high-class." Hannah accepted her glass of wine and smiled approvingly. "Me likey."

"And you didn't want to come." I licked my lips, which had gone dry. *Jesus, I can't even say the word "come."*

Hannah wrinkled her nose. "Baby? Are you okay?"

The therapist's words came back to me. *"Go away for the weekend, have a glass of wine, then have sex."*

I put my glass down untouched. "I'm good."

"Are you…" Hannah's voice trailed off, and she looked unsure. "Hungry?"

I stood up immediately, and my stupid thighs screamed again. "Starving."

"Okay. Just let me get changed, and we can go eat in the bar?"

I kissed her forehead, yearning for so much more—but simultaneously feeling like I was dodging a bullet. "It's a date."

Chapter 18

HANNAH

I knew what was bothering Wes, even if he didn't want to say it.

He had stage fright. Sexy-hotel stage fright.

It takes one to know one.

Taking a deep breath, I gathered my courage. I changed into skintight, black faux-leather pants (which were vegan) and a low-cut tank top, making sure my lacy bra was visible underneath. I put on extra mascara and dotted my lips with gloss. For the finale, I shook my hair loose so it hung it waves, the way Wes liked it, and put on sky-high spiked heels.

I looked ready for…date night. Date night with my big,sexy boyfriend, who I could tell needed me to hold his hand tonight and let him know everything was going to be okay.

But everything was *not* okay when I went back to the bedroom. Wes took one look at me and put a hand over his heart, clutching it.

I rushed to him. "Oh my God, Wes!"

His face was red. "Babe, you look so hot—my heart stopped."

I clutched him with one hand and put the other over my own heart. "So you're not having tachycardia?"

Wes chuckled and pulled me against his massive chest, careful not to smudge my makeup. "No—I mean, maybe, but it's the best tachycardia *ever*."

After I was certain he wasn't about to have a heart attack, I swatted him.

He grinned, pulling me close as we headed out the door.

I relished the feel of his big body—even though I was five foot eight and wearing three-inch heels, he made me feel dainty and protected. "Do Brian and the other guys have to come to dinner, too?"

He shrugged. "They'll sit at the other end of the bar. We can send them a drink."

We sat at a secluded table in the corner, while Brian and the other guards sipped seltzer and watched the area like hawks. I perused the menu, which was fabulous. "I think I'm going to have the asparagus salad and the black cod with the dry miso rub. What looks good to you, babe?"

Wes peered at me over the top of his menu. "Do you want the truth?"

"Of course."

"The rib eye."

I scowled at the menu. "You mean, the *twenty-ounce* rib eye with the béarnaise sauce?"

Wes looked at me pleadingly. "That's the one."

I giggled. "So order it, silly. Just make sure you don't eat any other red meat this week! You need to be heart-healthy."

He threw his menu down and smiled. It was like the sun coming out. "You're the best, babe."

I smiled back, even if I didn't approve of the steak. "So are you."

* * *

After predinner cocktails and sharing a bottle of wine, Wes and I felt no pain as we headed back to our suite. We waved to Brian and the other guards. "Don't wait up," Wes joked.

Brian offered us a rare smile. "Good night, you two. We got you covered."

I complained about having security, but it *was* nice to know that we didn't have to worry about you-know-who…

I pushed the thought from my mind as we headed inside, and then all of a sudden, we were alone again, and I was a bundle of throbbing, frazzled nerves. But not about you-know-who; about you-know-*what*.

I licked my lips as I watched Wes strip out of his polo shirt and dark jeans. His muscles rippled, and even though I agreed his physical therapist was Evil Spawn, she *had* been effective.

He smiled when he caught me staring. "Are you checking me out?"

I twisted a lock of my hair. "Yes."

He came over and pulled me against him. "If I didn't say it before, you look beautiful tonight."

"You did say it—but thank you again."

His blue eyes flashed as he ran his hands down my body. "And I love the pants, by the way. Very hot."

"Thank you." I sucked in a deep breath as he gently cupped my ass. "They're fake leather. Vegan, in case you were wondering."

He arched an eyebrow and laughed. "Vegan leather pants? Now I've heard everything."

I buried my face in his chest and giggled, too, but it was more from nerves than anything else.

He could sense it immediately. "Hey." He removed his hands from my ass and gently kissed the top of my head. "We don't have to do this tonight. We can just go to sleep."

I looked up and straight into his eyes, so kind and concerned. "Oh, we are doing this tonight."

He crushed his lips against mine, and I shuddered in pleasure as our tongues connected, lazily at first, then growing in urgency.

I was breathing hard when we finally broke apart. "We are *so* doing this. Get on the bed, big boy."

Wes held up his hands in mock surrender, biceps bulging, and headed for the bed. Once he was settled, I turned on some music and slowly stripped off my clothes, letting him watch. I felt a little self-conscious, but I wanted him to know that I wanted him badly, and that I was ready. Because I was *so* ready. I don't know if it was the crazy light machine or telling him what had really happened to me or if it had just been enough time, but I was done with waiting. I needed him. I needed to feel him inside me.

I headed to the bed and straddled him. He was already rock hard, ready for me, and I sucked in a deep breath as I pressed myself against him. *Do I still know how to do this?*

He stroked my face gently, gazing into my eyes. "Baby? Are you sure?"

In that moment, all the fear and anxiety fell away—because I knew in my heart that if I said no or showed the slightest hesitation, he would be fine. *We* would be fine.

"I'm sure. Wes, I need to tell you something."

"Babe?"

"I love you. I love you so much."

"You do?"

I nodded, feeling solemn. "I wish I'd told you sooner."

His eyes looked like they filled with tears for a second, but he gave a manly cough and they were gone. "I love you, too."

I grinned. "You do?"

"I wish I'd told you sooner, too."

He sat up straighter to kiss me, but I didn't miss the flash of pain on his face. "Wesley Eden, you're still hurting," I scolded.

"I'll live. But not without you," he growled, and crushed his lips against mine again.

He sank his big hands into my hair. Our kiss quickly turned urgent, and I moaned as he deepened it. I pulled back, a little breathless, and asked, "Can we switch places?"

He tenderly brushed the hair back from my face. "We can do whatever you want."

I rolled off of him and onto my back. Wes knew I thought the missionary position was the most romantic, and I wanted to feel his big body covering mine. He made me feel safe.

He gently placed himself on top of me, keeping his weight on his arms. His muscles strained, and I wondered if this was too much on him, but then he kissed me again, and I could feel his erection throbbing between my legs, and all I could think about was getting him inside me.

"I can tell you're worried about me—don't be. I'd stop if I felt like I needed to."

I let out the deep breath I hadn't known I'd been holding. "Okay."

Another thing I could let go: worrying about him breaking.

Wes trailed kisses down my neck, and I sighed in relief and pleasure. Relief showed on his own face as he kissed me, ecstatically moving down to my breasts. He grunted in pure pleasure as he took one of my nipples in his mouth, kissing it reverently.

Then he stopped and smiled. "Oh my God, I'm in heaven."

I arched my back and moaned, begging for more.

I was wet now, aching for him. All the things I'd worried I wouldn't be able to feel? I felt them, lighting up under Wes's touch, his tender caresses and enormous, chiseled body. I didn't think about anything but Wes and his rippling muscles and protruding manhood and *having him inside me right now.*

And the fact that he loved me back.

I slid my sex against his—his erection was thick, heavy, and wet at the tip, ready for me.

He slid my panties off and his body covered mine, protecting me from the rest of the world, claiming me. He kissed me again until we were both breathless and I felt dizzy. His erection rubbed against me, his body slick with my wetness. "Are you ready?"

"Yes." He tenderly kissed me again. I ached against him—feeling overwhelmed with love and with longing.

I put my hands on his firm ass and guided him against my wet heat. He entered me slowly, inch by thick, marvelous inch.

We both sighed when he was all the way in. It felt *so* good.

He held my face gently in his hands as he began to thrust. I laughed and groaned in pleasure at the same time. Wes was *huge*, and I always felt like I was about to come as soon as he was inside me. This was no different. I cried out as he pumped his hips, absolute joy coursing through me because we were back together, bodies entwined.

"I missed this so much." The cords in his neck stood out as he propped himself up with his arms.

I ran my hands down his chiseled chest, tracing one of his scars. He had got that from me, from protecting me.

He would've given his life for me, and he still would. I knew it.

But instead of feeling sad for that fact, or guilty, I felt grateful. *I would do it for him, too.*

I closed my eyes and opened myself up under him—all of me, my heart, my body, my soul. Relief coursed through me as I felt him love me, fierce and tender all at the same time. And when his thrusts got more insistent and I heard him moan, my body throbbed around his. I begged him to come inside me, to fill me.

"I'm not gonna last, babe—"

But I started to unravel then, my cries drowning him out. The orgasm hit me hard, tearing through me, blocking everything else out except the feel of him inside me, of our bodies fused together. Wes fucked me hard through my orgasm. Then he moaned and came in a torrent, his hot seed filling me, pushing me over the edge again. I cried out as my vision blurred, my body pulsing around his cock, greedily sucking him dry.

I don't know when we stopped. I don't know when I stopped yelling. All I knew was, when I finally came to, we were collapsed together in a sweaty pile of limbs and Wes was already snoring.

I gently pushed him off me, and he blearily opened one eye. "That was amazing. I love you so much." He smiled at me—groggy, satisfied, and cocky.

I beamed at him. "It *was* amazing. And I love you more."

He nestled me against his massive chest and kissed me. "G'night."

Then he immediately started snoring again, and I giggled against him, feeling safe, warm, and utterly loved. "Good night."

* * *

WES

I was so psyched. My dick *totally* still worked.

Just to make sure, I asked Hannah if she wanted to check out the plunge pool the next morning.

She grinned at me, her hair wild and her skin glowing. "Uh, *yeah*. Of course I do."

I picked her up and carried her outside.

She bit her lip, looking worried. "Are you sure you should be doing this—carrying me?"

I beamed down at her, relishing the feel of having her in my arms, her legs wrapped around my midsection. I was sore, I wasn't back to normal yet, but I felt reinvigorated.

"Yep. After last night, I feel like I could do anything. But you know what we *forgot* to do…" My first thought this morning? *Holy shit, we went bareback!*

But the idea made me excited, not nervous. Maybe nervous-excited.

"I know," Hannah groaned. "We totally got caught up in the moment! But it should be okay. Where I'm at in my cycle—I don't think we need to freak out."

"I'm not freaking out." I grinned at her. "I freaking love you, though."

She grinned back. "I freaking love you, too." She started to say something, but stopped herself.

"What?"

"What if we, you know..."

"What if I knocked you up?" I kissed her sweet lips. "Then you and I will have a beautiful baby together." I put her down gently and took off my shirt. Hannah's eyes traveled appreciatively up and down my torso.

Just like that, my dick got rock hard. *Yes.* I mentally fist pumped—*confirmed!* I slid her T-shirt off and admired her pale, perfect skin in the sunlight.

She leaned forward and whispered, "Should we really be out here *naked*?"

I looked around the private courtyard, secluded by a high wall. "Absolutely."

Hannah's cheeks reddened as she eyed the small pool. "Won't they hear us?"

I grinned at her. "Only if you scream your head off." Which she totally would—a point of pride with me. I loved that she was loud. Her unabashed appreciation for our sex was a total turn-on.

"I'll try to keep it down." Her face flushed as she eyed my erection. "If I can."

I laced my fingers through hers. "We can go back inside if you want."

"No." She leaned up on her tiptoes to kiss me, and the yearning I felt in her kiss made my heart somersault. I delved my hands into her blonde hair, pulling her against me as our tongues connected, sending zigzags of desire rippling through my body.

She pulled back and led me to the pool. Her self-consciousness of moments before disappeared. She stripped out of her panties and stepped languidly into the pool, which was totally sexy right up until she got in deeper and yelped, "It's so cold!"

I chuckled and stripped out of my boxers. I climbed down into the pool, the cold water bracing against my thighs, my erection bobbing in front of me, determined to warm her up.

Hannah lifted herself up and sat on the edge of the pool, shivering, but with her legs spread open slightly to expose her glistening sex. I kissed her mouth, my hands traveling down her body, my thumbs stroking her perfect, pink nipples, which hardened under my touch.

"So beautiful." My voice was a low growl.

Her skin grew hot underneath my touch.

Our kiss deepened, and she moaned as I slid my hand down to her sex, my fingers lazily circling her clit. Impatient, she moved against me so my hand ground against her harder. Then she cried out, already forgetting her vow of silence.

I chuckled, loving her impatience, loving *her*. Was it only yesterday we'd been skittish around each other and I'd been a nervous wreck about this?

It felt so good to be back I was already about to burst as the cool water lapped at me, my hand on Hannah's blazing-hot, wet slit. She threw back her head and moaned as I stroked her, then leaned down and put my face between her legs.

She cried out as I licked her from her slit up to her clit.

"Oh, baby." She slid her fingers into my hair. "I need you…"

I needed her, too, but I didn't want to tear myself away from her glorious body. I needed her to know that I loved her, that she was *mine*, that I owned every inch of her body to honor, protect, and pleasure. I continued to lap at her clit, sucking it hard as she writhed beneath me. I put one finger gently inside her. She was already so wet, I slid in another, and then proceeded to thrust in and out as I nibbled and sucked on her clit.

She threw her head back again, moaning, an orgasm immediately tearing through her body. "Wes. *Wes!*"

Pure satisfaction coursed through me as I continued to thrust with my fingers and kiss her hotly, bringing her through the orgasm and to the other side.

She sat up, her body trembling, but she reached for me. "I need you." She kissed me deeply, running her hands down my face and body, making me feel like the luckiest bastard in the entire world. This time I remembered. I grabbed a condom from where I'd tossed it, next to the pool, and rolled it on.

She spread her legs again and guided my shaft against her. She took my face in her hands as I notched myself inside her and entered her slowly.

Her blue eyes sparkled with emotion as she held my face, our gazes level. "I love you so much."

I leaned into her, my heart about to burst. "I love you more. I will forever."

"Oh, Wes."

And with that—the early morning sun shining down on us, our bodies fused together—we moved forward into our future.

Chapter 19

HANNAH

He brushed the hair back from my face. "Everyone in the house totally heard *that*. People in Canada heard that."

"No way." I tried to swat him, but my limbs were too weak.

"Yes, way."

"Wes?" I asked, after a minute.

"Yes?"

"I was thinking. You might need a plunge pool at the new house." I giggled.

"I can arrange that." Wes looked pleased with himself, just like he had all weekend.

Even though we were back home, we were still…busy. And he hadn't stopped smiling or having his way with me. The memories from the weekend flooded me, making me feel sexy. *Again*. I moved toward him, trailing my fingers down his chest suggestively, my skin already heating up.

Wes knew exactly what I wanted. He laughed, then squinted at the clock. "You can't seriously want to do that again!"

I giggled. "I *do*, but I should probably go to work."

He pulled me closer and nuzzled my neck. "If you really want to go again, I'm in. Call in sick."

"I can't." I continued to trace his chiseled chest. "My boss will know I'm faking."

Wes shook his head. "I hope they didn't hear us just now—but I bet they did."

"They didn't—they couldn't! This is a freaking mansion. We have our own wing."

He propped himself up and stared at me. "You're *loud*."

My face reddened. "I can't help it if you make me scream."

That cocky grin lit up his face, the one I'd missed. "Don't get me wrong—I love it. But I bet somebody heard you."

"No way."

He arched an eyebrow. "We'll see."

"Want to push our luck?" I climbed on top of him.

* * *

First thing Monday morning, Lauren eyed me over her mug of coffee. "Uh, everything okay?"

I beamed at her. "Everything's great."

She laughed.

"What?"

"I'm guessing your skin isn't glowing from a spa facial this weekend. And have you seen your hair yet this morning?" She handed me a coffee.

I took a grateful sip, then patted my hair. It felt like a rat's nest. "No, why?"

"It's a little wild." She looked at me knowingly. "It sounded like…things…" She cleared her throat. "*Things* meaning your weekend…were still getting a little wild, too."

I coughed, almost spitting out my coffee. "You did not just reference sex in a conversation with me."

"Did so."

"My virgin-prude sister is talking to me about sex?"

Lauren stuck out her tongue. "I'm engaged now. I haven't been a virgin prude in quite some time—and last night, it sounded like you hadn't been, either. Not to mention this morning."

I shook my head and drank more coffee. "Never ever in a million years did I think you'd be able to have a conversation like this with a straight face."

She shrugged. "I've loosened up. A little."

"Well, good. It's about time!"

Her expression turned serious. "Was everything all right?"

I hadn't told her much, but my sister knew me well. I grinned.

"You heard me. It was more than all right." I grabbed my coffee to go. "I need to get ready for work now, Miss Nosy Pants."

"Okay, see you at the office…and if you happen to bump into Wes while you're getting dressed, try to keep it down!"

* * *

"Leo gave me these for you to look at." Lauren dumped a stack of files on my desk.

I opened them, surprised to find numerous pictures of Jiàn Innovations employees, along with brief bios. "What's this?"

"You said we needed an informant inside Li Na's company. These are the potential candidates," Lauren said.

My stomach flipped. "You're *agreeing* with me?"

She shrugged. "I'm agreeing it will make it easier for us to ascertain whether or not Li Na has fallen for the false prototype I'm uploading to our system early next week. I also want to track the status of the Protocol technology."

My jaw dropped. "You're really almost ready with the false prototype?"

She arched an eyebrow. "It isn't one hundred percent yet. But Li Na doesn't know that. I'm done screwing around with her, and I like your plan. I think it has…legs."

"You *like* my plan? Since when?"

Lauren smiled as she headed for the door. "Since I took the weekend to think it through and feel certain that what we're doing is for the greater good. So look through those files. Find someone we can intimidate without crossing a line of criminal threatening. I'd like to keep my baby sister out of jail long enough to be my maid of honor, thank you very much."

I stood up. "Wait! Does that mean you've picked a date?"

It looked like I wasn't the only one who'd been busy this weekend.

"First things first—let's get the corporate terrorist out of our lives, then I'll get married, okay?"

That sounded promising…if I could deliver on my plan. My palms started to sweat. "Okay."

Lauren stuck her head back in. "And Hannah? I'm counting on you. I know you can do this."

I blinked at my sister, who never so much as delegated an email. She was trusting me to flesh out the plan and make Li Na go away, once and for all.

"I won't let you down."

Her face softened. "Don't worry. You never do."

* * *

The rest of the week passed in a blur. Outside of work, I'd attended therapy and EMDR, started running again, met Fiona for yoga, and helped Wes begin a search for a new house. We'd also consummated our relationship approximately nine thousand more times. At Paragon, I'd been busy catching up with meetings, reviewing Lauren's proposed prototype, and researching different blackmail candidates within Jiàn Innovations. I'd also thrown myself into updating my list of the best international healthcare business news outlets—when the time came, I wanted the truth about Li Na Zhao heralded around the globe.

Poised to strike, I headed to Lauren's office, where I paced with my arms crossed tight against my chest. "I think I found someone we can use, but you're not going to like my reasoning."

"Who is it?" she asked.

"Biyu Lin—Lin Biyu—in China the name order is reversed, so it's technically Lin Biyu."

Jittery with adrenaline, I grabbed her file and opened it on Lauren's desk. Biyu's pretty face stared up at me from her corporate photo, and a stab of guilt pierced my chest.

Lauren studied the photograph, frowning. "Why did you pick her? What am I not going to like?"

"I chose her because she got divorced recently and she has a young son."

Lauren dropped the picture, her eyeballs bugging out of her head. "*That's* your criteria?"

I nodded, twisting my bracelet. "She's vulnerable. She needs money."

"How do you know that?"

I kept twisting. "She started at Jiàn Innovations three months ago. She's never held a corporate job before—she's been home with her son. I had Leo do some digging, and public records indicate she got divorced right before she started at the company. She also moved to an apartment in a neighborhood where rent is cheap. Dave checked her bank account, which indicates she's living paycheck to paycheck."

Lauren looked appalled. "So you want to target a young, single, broke mother?"

"She works directly underneath Li Na's top executive assistant. She'll have access, although not as much as I'd like. The other reason I chose her is that she has a dual degree in English and computer science, so not only can we can communicate, she'll be proficient with any technical requests I have."

My sister looked at me as if I'd sprouted three heads. "What exactly are you planning?"

I went to the window and stared out at the grounds, reminding myself of what we were fighting for, even as my heart pounded. "I'm going to have Dave and Leo set up a fake email address so I can contact her. I'll tell her I'm doing… market research. I'll offer her money in exchange for information and see if she's going to be cooperative."

"What if she says no?"

"Then I'll have to be more persuasive."

"What if she runs to her boss? Or the police?" Lauren asked.

"I'll let her know that's not a great idea."

"Because…?"

I didn't move from the window. "Because if she tells anyone, she could be putting herself in danger. Or someone she loves."

"*What* did you just say?"

I turned to face her. "You heard me—and you know I don't mean it. But I need to motivate her and also keep her quiet. We need this information from Jiàn. We need to know if they're taking the bait. Think of all the bad things Li Na's done—all the people she's hurt. We need to stop her, Lauren!"

Lauren shook her head, clearly not agreeing. "But this low-level administrative assistant has done nothing. She's a victim here, too."

I sighed. "I know that. I'm not going to do anything to hurt her, and I won't let anything bad happen to her either."

"How can you promise that? What if Li Na finds out? There's no one in Shenzhen who can protect this poor woman if that happens."

"Wes and Ellis both worked in China while they were in the military. Wes doesn't know anyone deployed there anymore, but Ellis said he still has a few contacts. If I need emergency help, I can get it."

Lauren didn't look convinced. "No offense, but that seems a little tangential."

"I know—but hopefully it won't be necessary." I started to pace. "Biyu has to keep this a secret. That's why threatening her makes sense, even though it makes me sick. She won't do anything to put her child in jeopardy."

Lauren sat down heavily. "I can't believe we're even considering this. After what Li Na's done to us, to Fiona…we should take the high road. This is *not* who we are."

"Of course it's not. But think of it this way—we're trying to prevent another tragedy." I'd known Lauren wouldn't like the idea—there was nothing to like about it. Still, we needed an ally in place if any of this was going to work. "Li Na ordered a hit on Jim Pace. She had Wes shot, she kidnapped me, and she killed Clive Warren. Don't forget that she had you and Timmy locked up, too. Thank God he saved you."

Li Na had held my sister and her longtime bodyguard prisoner during her first attempt to acquire the patch. Lauren had outsmarted her and escaped, but not before Timmy had to kill several guards in order to protect my sister.

Lauren tucked a strand of hair behind her ear. "I remember—I was there. But it doesn't justify our sinking to the same level."

"We're not. I am trying to *avoid* more people getting hurt. Wes keeps offering to go to China, to take care of Li Na himself. Do you think I want that? After what he's been through?"

Her shoulders slumped. "Of course not."

I stepped closer to my sister. "You know I don't believe in violence—I hate it. I'm going to threaten this woman, but I'm doing it for her own good. I won't do anything to disappoint you, but we need to make this work."

"Fine," Lauren said. "Just promise me one thing."

"Anything."

She raised her gaze to meet mine. "That I recognize you when this is all over. And that you won't do anything you'll regret."

"Fine," I said.

Lauren smoothed her hair. "Fine."

But I wondered as I headed to my sunny, cheerful office…could this actually turn out *fine*?

Back at my desk, I sent Leo and Dave a text.

Set up the email account. I'm contacting Biyu today.

10-4, Dave wrote back. A few minutes later, he sent me a link to the account.

Taking a deep breath, I drafted an email to Biyu Lin, wondering if I was about to ruin her life.

Chapter 20

WES

Even though Hannah objected, I went to the big meeting at Paragon.

"I need to keep up with what's going on. I'm back to work, remember? Just on restricted duty."

Levi and I had finalized the paperwork this week—I was now officially a Betts Security employee.

She frowned as she stalked through the hallway to the conference room, with me close on her heels. "What exactly does 'restricted duty' mean?"

"It means I can go to meetings. It means I'm filling out paperwork and attending training sessions so I'm ready for active assignments. But I'm not actually doing anything I enjoy, like shooting bad guys."

Her eyes flashed. "Your shooting days are over, big guy."

I held open the door for her, admiring the way her dress showed off her legs even though she was being ridiculous. My shooting-bad-guys days were far from over. I tore my eyes away from her and cased the room; I didn't have to be on active duty to protect her. But all I found near the conference table were the usual suspects—Lauren, Gabe, Dave, Leo, Levi, Asher, Bethany, and Ellis standing protectively near Fiona.

Lauren motioned us toward the table. "Have a seat. I'm just reviewing a couple of things before I start."

Hannah made a beeline for Fiona, hugged her hard, then grabbed the empty seat next to Bethany. I clapped Ellis on the shoulder and found my own seat.

Bethany and Hannah chatted for a minute, eagerly catching up. Then Bethany's sharp eyes traveled over to me, taking in my dress shirt and laptop.

"So," she asked Hannah, keeping her voice low, "both you *and* Wes are completely back to work? I thought he was still doing rehab."

"I'm back full-time, but Wes is on *restricted duty*. He sort of excused himself from his wheelchair." Hannah made sure she said it pointedly, so I could hear.

"But you guys are good?" Bethany asked.

"Yeah—we're great."

I could hear the grin in Hannah's voice.

"Aw, that's wonderful." Bethany clapped her hands together. "I'm so happy for you that you finally met the right guy. He's got that big, protective, kick-ass thing going on—I totally get it."

Even though I was pretending not to listen, I couldn't help but puff my chest out.

"What's new with you?" Hannah asked. "How's having a bodyguard?"

"Randy's fine. He does what I tell him." Bethany lowered her voice. "It's *Levi* who's driving me nuts."

"What's going on?"

"He won't stop checking on me. He offered to personally protect my house. He *asked me to dinner*."

Hannah laughed, but when Bethany glared at her, she disguised it as a cough. "The nerve."

Bethany arched an eyebrow. "I don't have time for dinner, not with a thug."

Hannah motioned across the conference table to Levi, who was checking messages on his phone and studiously not looking at Bethany. "He's not a thug—that's an Armani suit he's wearing."

"He's pretty, I'll give him that much." Bethany frowned as she shot a look Levi's way. "But you know how I feel about dating. After Tony, I'm done. Fool me once, fine. But I'll never be fooled again."

"Just because Tony was an ass doesn't mean you have to be alone forever."

Hannah had mentioned that Bethany was divorced, and that it had been nasty.

Bethany tapped her pen against the table. "I think it does. Besides, I'm too busy to date. I had *fifty* billable hours last week. Who has time for dinner?"

Hannah looked as if she was going to argue further, but Lauren cleared her throat. "Sorry for the delay. Let's get started."

She turned on her laptop and faced the room. "You all know why we're here. We've decided to go after Li Na Zhao preemptively, before she attacks us again. My sister deserves credit for coming up with this campaign—she's the brains behind this operation."

Lauren smiled while Hannah blushed.

"This is the prototype I uploaded to Paragon's server earlier today," Lauren continued, turning on the projector and adjusting the image. "It's for a sensor that tracks unusual metastasizing of cells. The potential customers are patients who are in remission from cancer who need to monitor the growth of their cells on an ongoing basis. If you look here"—she zoomed in to the center of the device, which looked like some sort of microchip—"you can see the 'brains' of this device. Similar to the patch, this is its sensor, which analyzes the data stream on a constant basis. This technology is different from what's already available because it's implanted directly into the patient and can continually monitor cell activity once it's in place."

Lauren took a sip of water. "The problem with this chip, what you can't see from the prototype, is that although this technology will produce a stream of information, it will only be partially correct. There's a timing lag, a disconnect between what the sensors are actually seeing and what they're reporting. But the defect isn't obvious unless you know exactly what you're looking for."

"So it looks like it works, but the reporting's actually faulty?" Fiona asked.

"Exactly." Lauren motioned to the image on the screen. "I uploaded all the specs to the server today, and I had legal working around the clock to prepare patent and preliminary FDA filings. But those regulatory documents are fakes."

Bethany scowled. "Legal prepared *fake* FDA documents?"

Lauren nodded.

"Why didn't you run this by me first?"

Lauren just raised an eyebrow as if Bethany's tone explained everything.

Bethany scribbled furiously in her notebook, muttering to herself. I thought I caught the words *ungrateful*, *reckless*, and *sneaky*, but I couldn't be sure.

Lauren ignored her. "Li Na's watched me for years, and she knows that I don't make FDA applications lightly. I believe she'll take the bait. Once she does, I *know* she'll try to rush this to market and blow through the Chinese regulatory process. I'm betting that Li Na and her team won't see the problem, they'll just see the results—and that will be good enough for them."

Gabe raised his hand. "Are you going to tell the board of directors about this?"

Paragon's long-suffering board of directors had overseen the company through corporate espionage, murder of a former board member, internal treason, kidnappings, hackings, and other nefarious activities. Their collective heads were probably spinning.

Lauren sighed. "No. They've been too close to our more...*er*, questionable activity over the past year. I'm shielding them and letting them sit this one out. You are, too," she told Gabe. "So if Allen Trade asks you to play golf, tell him you're busy."

Allen Trade was the board's president and a friend of Gabe's.

Apparently, Allen wasn't invited to this particular party. Gabe shrugged. "Probably for the best."

Bethany scribbled something else into her notebook, then raised her hand. "Is this technology something you want to pursue when this is over?"

An unexpected smile broke out over Lauren's face. "It's more promising than I initially thought. It's years away from being market-ready, but I believe we've found Paragon's next big hit."

Leo raised his hand, and Lauren motioned for him to speak. "Once we've confirmed that Li Na's copied the files, we'll monitor the situation closely. I think the main concern is making sure the product doesn't actually get to market in this condition."

Hannah cleared her throat. "But we need to be sure that Li Na's proceeding and planning to fast-track it to market."

"How will we know that?" Bethany asked.

"I have a source inside Jiàn Innovations." Hannah's voice was quiet but clear. "This person will keep us up-to-date on what's happening."

Ash whistled. "Nice."

Bethany tapped her pen, looking less than pleased again. "How exactly did we get a source?"

Hannah shot Lauren a look, then turned to Bethany. "I reached out to them. They were happy to help."

"*Happy?*" Bethany stopped tapping. "I'm not really getting a 'happy' vibe from any of this."

"Let's talk later," Hannah said quickly.

"I have an update." Fiona looked pulled together in an elegant black sheath, but there were dark circles beneath her eyes. "My attorneys have signed off on the license agreement with Jiàn. They've been in contact with Li Na's legal team. We're ready to finalize the paperwork."

"Why did you do a license agreement?" Levi asked.

"I didn't think Li Na would believe that I'd changed my mind one hundred percent about selling the company. An exclusive license allows Protocol to retain rights over the therapy, but Jiàn will be able to begin manufacturing and distribution if the Chinese government gives them the green light. Which I believe they will, much faster than we'll get final approval in the US."

Fiona lined her phone up neatly with her laptop. "But the technology Li Na gets won't work correctly. The initial specs are legitimate, but once they're in Jiàn's servers, we are going to attack them with destructive code. Leo and Dave have reverse-engineered the virus Li Na tried to insert into Paragon's servers a few weeks ago. If the virus makes it past Jiàn's firewalls, no one will be able to detect it. Li Na will think everything is fine, but the virus will target Protocol Therapeutics's files, rewriting some of them. Once she goes to pull the trigger with the new technology, it will malfunction."

"So we're letting her steal technology that doesn't work, and we're selling her technology that's defective," Levi said. "That's all great, but how is this ruining her again? Because I'd like to get that part."

"Since it's clear that she won't be extradited any time soon and we don't want to send Betts personnel to physically harm her, we've decided to ruin her professional life, which is all she appears to care about."

Lauren motioned to Hannah, who took the floor.

"Li Na's been very vocal about what she and her company can do for Shenzhen. She will brag about these technologies, making sure every person in biotech knows that she's bringing two new amazing cancer products to market. Trust me, this is what she's been waiting for, and she will make a *colossal* deal about this."

Hannah tucked a lock of hair behind her ear and continued. "Which is where I come in—I've been in touch with my contacts, feeding them tidbits about a huge biotech story that I know is coming down the pipeline. I'm generating excitement and curiosity. Once Li Na moves forward, her own publicity team will move into high gear. There's going to be a lot of buzz.

"I'll tip my contacts that the Jiàn Innovations story is the Next Big Thing—and that I have special industry-insider information. I'll work them up into a frenzy. The whole world will be watching her. And when the launches backfire, she'll fail catastrophically, and even better, she'll fail in public. Li Na's reputation will be in shambles, and Jiàn Innovations will be a cautionary tale taught in B-school. Done and done!"

Levi grinned. "I like it."

"I like it, too." But Hannah didn't smile back. "I'll like it better when it works."

After the meeting wrapped up, Fiona, Hannah, and Lauren began to talk. I took the opportunity to approach Ellis. "How's it going?"

"Good." His eyes kept roaming to Fiona and sweeping the rest of the room, on high alert.

"I think we're safe in here."

His blue eyes snapped back to me. "We're safe until we aren't."

"I heard Fiona's moving forward with this plan because she feels like her family is safe. You're doing a great job. Congrats."

Ellis frowned. "I don't really think congratulations are in order."

We grimaced at each other. I loved my brother, but he could be the consummate buzzkill.

Hannah waved us over. "Fiona and I need to talk more—we're going to grab lunch at Mado before she heads back to the office. Do you guys want to come?"

"Love to."

Ellis nodded, too—it wasn't as if he'd let Fiona out of his sight.

Mado was the hottest new restaurant in Palo Alto, and I was pretty sure they didn't serve Bud in a bottle. I chuckled to myself as we headed out, wondering what in hell my brother was going to order.

The restaurant was packed with the typical Silicon Valley crowd—men wearing those odd fabric shoes that were the hot new thing, and of course the jeans, T-shirts, and hoodies that were iconic markers of our geographic location. The women were more varied; some in dresses, some in sweaters, but mostly in neutral colors. Silicon Valley wasn't particularly stylish, but there still seemed to be a dress code, and people trying to identify as part of the tribe.

The clothes might not be fashionable, but Mado was. There was a Mado in New York, London, and LA. The fact that Palo Alto had gotten one meant we'd arrived.

We sat down in our booth, and Ellis scowled at the menu. He didn't look particularly enthused about the destination.

"This looks amazing." Hannah scanned the lunch options. "I think I'm going to try the crispy Brussel sprouts and the tuna-sashimi tacos."

"Sounds great," Fiona said. "I'm going to get the same, except I'm getting the edamame appetizer."

Hannah smiled in approval. "I've heard it's delicious."

Ellis watched them as if he were waiting for the punchline.

I tapped his menu. "What are you going to order?"

"Uh…"

Fiona leaned forward. "You might like the short ribs—they're marinated in soy sauce, so they're pretty normal."

Ellis offered her a rare smile. "Thanks. Normal sounds good." But a scowl crept over his face as he watched the busy bar area. "Wes. At the bar."

The tone in his voice told me to turn around cautiously.

I scanned the busy lounge, unsure of what had him on alert. "Who're you looking at?"

Ellis straightened himself. "The guy in the gray fleece hoodie. I've seen him before—this week, but I can't place it." My brother cursed under his breath.

I watched the man. He had broad shoulders and short hair, and blended into the crowd with his uniform of sweatshirt, jeans, and Chuck Taylor sneakers. But I could tell from his posture that he knew how to handle himself, and also that he was carrying concealed.

"Fuck," I said, unceremoniously, making the women jump.

"What is it?" Hannah asked.

I took her hand and squeezed it. "Nothing you need to worry about. I got you."

"We're being followed." Ellis moved slightly, putting his body a fraction in front of Fiona in case he had to shield her. "Don't get upset. He doesn't know we've seen him. We're just going to sit here and eat like we planned. He doesn't seem like he's going to shoot us—he's just doing surveillance."

I whipped out my phone. "I'll text Brian and have him do a full check outside to make sure there's no one else."

As I tapped out the urgent message, Hannah shuddered and Fiona went pale. "Don't worry. Wes and I will take care of him." Ellis kept his voice low, soothing.

I kept Hannah close as my brother and I briefly locked his gazes, silently acknowledging the situation. We were both armed. Mr. Gray Hoodie didn't know we'd made him, and we could use that to our advantage.

We *would* use that to our advantage. I knew how my brother operated, back from when we were growing up. Whether it was hide-and-seek, a "friendly" game of neighborhood football, or capture the flag, Ellis and I were an unstoppable team, demolishing the other kids with our commitment and fierce determination to win.

Most of the time, the other kids quit or went home crying. Or both. *Weenies.*

"So, just act normal?" Fiona asked.

Ellis smiled again, clearly trying to keep things on an even keel. "Normal sounds good."

Fiona nodded, looking resigned. But she ordered wine when the server came.

My phone buzzed a minute later. "Brian said the lot's clear. He called for backups."

The muscle in Ellis's jaw jumped. "Perfect. We'll be ready."

"What does that mean?" Hannah scowled. "Wes isn't ready for a fight—he's on *restricted duty*."

She made it sound like I should be kept in a bubble.

"I'm fine." I squeezed her hand again. "And there's no way I'm letting anyone near you, babe. Not ever again. So don't fight me on this."

Hannah bit her lip, but sensing my urgency, said nothing.

Then she waved down our server and ordered wine, too.

Adrenaline thrummed through my body as we went through the motions of a sociable lunch. Ellis appeared relaxed and normal, actually leading the conversation at the table. He told Hannah and Fiona stories about our family, perking up as he went along.

His eyes sparkled as he told them about our favorite family pet, Moose the dog. "He used to howl every time this commercial for a certain doll came on. This big lug of a dog, howling over a little blonde doll with curls. Hysterical."

He cleaned his plate as he talked.

He never stopped scanning the room.

He ordered a chocolate bento box for dessert and ate that, too.

When he insisted on paying the check, I knew for sure he was enjoying himself.

Ellis couldn't wait to get his hands on Mr. Gray Hoodie. He was itching for a fight.

I already knew what he would say as we gathered our things and headed to the door.

"I'll take care of our friend—get Fiona and Hannah to the car. Have Brian bring them back to Gabe's."

"Why Gabe's?"

"Because he has a guesthouse filled with Betts Security agents," Ellis snapped. "I want Fiona safe while I call Levi and figure out what do with this guy."

He pretended to casually scroll through his phone, buying himself time as Mr. Gray Hoodie paid his check.

"Fine, but once I get them settled, I'm coming with you."

"I'll be at the other SUV."

One arm firmly around Hannah and one eye firmly on Fiona, I texted Brian. He drove up immediately, scanning the parking lot as he idled the SUV. Before the women could protest, I opened the back door and "helped" them inside—I offered Fiona my hand, which she accepted, but I had to practically shove Hannah inside the car.

She looked up at me balefully, clearly angry but also on the verge of tears. "I don't know why you're doing this." Her voice shook, and Fiona winced next to her.

"I'll be fine—it's no big deal." I leaned down and planted a firm kiss on her lips so she could feel how much I meant it.

"Can't you come with us instead?" she begged.

"I can't—I have to help Ellis." I hated to be separated from her, and Ellis would probably be just fine, but I wasn't going to miss out on the opportunity to find out more about the man who'd followed us. "Honestly? He isn't going to let me do much. He needs to flex his muscles."

"O-okay." Hannah tried to sound brave, but her eyes filled with tears. "But please be safe."

I turned to Brian, who looked annoyed by all the kissing and the crying. "We have four backup vehicles," he said. "Two for you and Ellis, two for me. I'll head back to Gabe's now and make sure Fiona and Hannah are safe."

"Thanks, Bri."

"Did you hear from Levi?"

"Not yet."

Brian put the SUV into Drive. "Okay, buddy. Please be safe."

In a rare attempt at humor, he fluttered his eyelashes, clearly imitating Hannah.

"Have I told you lately that you're sort of a dick?"

Brian grinned. "No."

"You're sort of a dick."

Hannah seconded that from the backseat.

Brian shrugged. "I know—sorry, Hannah. Wes, totally not sorry."

He sped off, taking my heart with him—and yeah, I knew what Brian would say to that. *Dick.* Sighing, I looked for my brother.

And then I realized I still had my heart—because it jumped into my throat when I spotted him across the parking lot, beating Mr. Gray Hoodie to a pulp in broad daylight.

Chapter 21

WES

I sprinted across the lot, almost collapsing by the time I reached them. I bent over to catch my breath. "*Stop.* This isn't open combat, it's the parking lot of a trendy restaurant. *Put him in the car.*"

Ellis punched the man one last time, grinning as Mr. Gray Hoodie's head lolled back. He tossed me the man's gun and stuffed him into the backseat, following close behind.

I cursed as I got behind the wheel. "We have two cars packed with agents watching us—you better hope they don't report you to Levi. He's not in the business of publicly beating people."

Ellis breathed hard, but he didn't look at all sorry. "*You* better hope I don't tell Hannah you ran at a full-out sprint."

I pulled out onto the road, eyeing him in the rearview mirror. He ignored me, inspecting the nearly passed-out man next to him, taking his wallet and examining his identification.

"Who do you work for?"

The man moaned.

Ellis put his Sig Sauer pistol against his temple. "Quit your crying. *Who do you work for?* You might as well tell me. It's not like they're going to come and rescue you from where you're going anyway."

The man cursed. "I don't know the client's name. I work for a service. All I know is the client's Chinese."

"Ding ding ding. We have a winner." Completely in his element, Ellis sounded gleeful.

"What're we going to do with this winner?" I asked.

Ellis's gaze met mine in the rearview mirror. "I haven't decided what I can use him for yet. I'll figure something out."

Unsure of what that meant, and unsettled by my brother's tone, I warily steered the car toward home.

* * *

LI NA

Once upon a time, Lauren Taylor bored me to tears. Her technology sparkled, but she was your typical American engineer: two-dimensional and obsessed with quantitative analysis. Such individuals were useful, but too narrow-minded for my taste.

I dated one once, at university.

I ended up giving him my virginity to shut him up about our mutual statistics class.

It was a good thing he'd been so well endowed. University would have been extremely boring otherwise, although I *had* enjoyed statistics.

I'd *almost* enjoyed it when Lauren blew up our last deal—finally, some colorful language. A spark rose to her surface. She'd exhibited some fight.

And then just this week…a new discovery. I'd assumed Lauren had continued to focus only on the patch, but during my regularly scheduled hack of Paragon's system, I'd found prototype plans for a new device. The plans were for a mini-sensor that monitored metastasizing cells using similar technology to the patch. If this prototype worked, it was going to revolutionize the cancer industry. The sensor would firmly cement Paragon as the world's leader in biotechnology.

Unless, of course, I appropriated the groundbreaking design and used it first.

I would have to move quickly. I watched Paragon's files daily, hacking in on a regular basis and monitoring for any new activity. The sensor's prototype, its supporting specs, and the related government filings were all uploaded to the system on the same day. I needed to understand why. Had Lauren been developing this privately? Was she about to begin clinical trials?

I had another thought. Her team hadn't been able to keep me out of their system. They had to know I watched them. Was Lauren Taylor trying to *play* me?

I thought back on that American engineer I'd dated. He didn't understand sarcasm or most humor. When I'd broken it off with him, he wanted a reason. I told him we lacked longterm potential, but that didn't compute. So I explained that statistically, we were at a disadvantage because not only were we an interracial couple, we were international—the empirical data indicated the likelihood of our success was miniscule. Pursuing the relationship would waste time that we could both put toward our studies or a relationship with better probabilities. Finally, he understood.

Did Lauren possess the ability to try to trick me? I didn't know if her brain could function that way—it seemed more the mark of a creative mind, one that didn't necessarily adhere to rigid rules and structures.

With only one way to find out, I'd copied all the new sensor's files.

My people were already working on a prototype based on the stolen files. I was busy preparing all the necessary documentation for a fast-track government approval process. The Chinese government understood the need to provide innovative medical technology to the public. An approval that would take months or years in the United States would be given in a matter of weeks.

In other breaking news, Fiona Pace had agreed to exclusively license her antibody therapy to me. It appeared her husband's untimely death had finally given her the proper motivation.

I'd say I was sorry, but I wasn't.

Pending government approval, which I would again receive in an expedited manner, Jiàn Innovations would announce its newest offering: the fastest cancer treatment therapy ever available. Because of the glacial pace at which the Federal Drug Administration moved, we would beat Protocol to market by a mile. I'd already begun the process of staffing a rollout, reaching out to distribution partners and prepping my facilities for an influx of orders.

Jiàn Innovations would launch two cutting-edge technologies this year. And then? All eyes would be on Shenzhen—and me. My prominence, already secured, would finally proliferate wildly.

Some would question my tactics, but I would stand by my results. In the end, I would help more people than I'd hurt. Men had done the same thing for centuries, declaring war in the name of their vision of a better world.

So, I reasoned, *let the weak wait.* If Lauren Taylor and Fiona Pace couldn't hear the clock ticking, I wouldn't waste my precious time screaming at them while they covered their ears.

* * *

HANNAH

Wes, Levi, and Ash were holed up in the guesthouse, busy interrogating the man we'd captured. Curious and not at all pleased by the day's events, Gabe and Lauren cornered me when they got home from work.

"What are they going to do with him?" Lauren asked.

I frowned as I laced up my sneakers. Running was the only way I could deal with such a stressful day. "I don't know."

Gabe cracked his knuckles. "I'm going to talk to Levi—I'm not sure I love the idea of keeping a hostage on my property."

Lauren kissed his cheek, looking stricken as he strode off. "Keep me posted."

She watched me as I started to stretch. "How was Fiona?"

"Nervous about the girls, of course. Ellis increased security at their property. He's not taking any chances."

She nodded. "Were you scared?"

"I was scared Wes was going to get hurt. He shouldn't be active yet." I bit my lip. "Honestly, I don't know if I can handle him going back on assignment after everything that's happened."

Lauren reached out and rubbed my arm. "Things will calm down eventually."

"He carries a concealed weapon for work. 'Calm' isn't really part of the job description."

"Have you asked him to think about doing something else?"

I shrugged. "Yes, but he loves his job. I don't think it's fair of me to push it."

"Can you live like this? Worrying about him?"

"I'll be fine. I just need to stay supportive." I couldn't ask Wes to give up his work—he helped people, and it was an important job. I just needed to toughen up. Plus, he'd never once asked me to walk away from Paragon, even though it had been chaotic and dangerous over the past year. "Other spouses do it. I can, too."

"Spouses?" Lauren asked eagerly, clearly trying to lighten the mood. "Do you have gossip?"

I put my hands on my hips. "Ugh, you know what I mean!"

She eyed my sneakers. "Do you want company?"

"Besides the three security guards who're going to follow me?" I eyed the guys, who were waiting in the entryway. "You're welcome to come, but I'll probably run a few hills."

Lauren grabbed her laptop and backed away. "I think I'll catch up on some reports. Come see me when you get back?"

"Sure." I headed to the entryway, collected my entourage, and headed outside. The roads surrounding Gabe's compound were quiet, with another occasional estate's driveway breaking up the woods. It was peaceful up here in the hills, and as soon as I started to jog, I calmed down.

I liked to run to music, the beat blaring and blocking out all thoughts. With one guard in front and two behind, I popped my headphones in and tried not to sing along—I didn't need to be hazed about my pathetic voice. Still, even with the drama of the day, I eventually settled into a pace and was able to let my thoughts fall away. After a mile, I felt better. I pumped my arms and breathed in the cool, late-afternoon air, thinking only of my next breath and putting one foot in front of the other.

Then my phone buzzed, pausing the music, and a notification flashed across my screen: finally, a response email from Biyu Lin.

I stopped running, heart pounding for a completely different reason.

I am not interested in what you proposed, she wrote. *Find someone else.*

I cursed—that wasn't the answer I'd been waiting for. I looked up, realizing the guys had stopped running and were waiting for me as I squinted at my phone and swore to myself.

"Sorry. I have to do a quick work email."

They busied themselves watching for threats and stretching their thighs.

I fired back an email to Biyu. *You don't want to say no to me. I could make your life difficult.*

I shook my head, trying to align my realities. Here I was, in beautiful, wildly upscale Northern California, firing off harassing messages while out for a run meant to clear my head. I looked down at myself—fluorescent, expensive running shoes, trendy Capri-length athletic tights, hot-pink tank top, and a ponytail stuck on top of my head. "Firework" by Katy Perry was positioned to blare next on my playlist. I wasn't in a position to threaten *anyone*—it wasn't my style.

Still, when Biyu emailed back, asking what I meant, I didn't hesitate. I needed to toughen up. For my sister, Wes, Fiona…for my own sake.

Help me or your family will suffer, like mine has, I wrote, hating myself for every word.

But that didn't stop me from hitting Send.

A few minutes later, she emailed me back, asking for detailed instructions. I couldn't help but smile. Because although I didn't like the method of travel, I was finally getting somewhere.

And I didn't plan on stopping until the final destination: freedom from Li Na Zhao.

CHAPTER 22

WES

"I can't believe you guys did this," Bethany hissed, standing outside the captive's room.

I shrugged. "We didn't have much choice."

Lauren must've told her what we'd done, because Bethany had stalked over from the main house, seething and intermittently complaining as we waited for Levi to come out of the interrogation room.

After a week of interrogation, our captive had finally told us his name was Carey, but I didn't believe him. His license and other documents were all fake. We had no idea who he really was or who'd paid him to follow Fiona—and he wouldn't talk.

Bethany snorted. "You didn't *have* to take him captive. Of *course* you had a choice."

"He'd been following Ellis and Fiona. Did you want us to wait until he attacked?"

"Did you want to call the *police* instead of assaulting him in public, then taking him hostage and keeping him locked up for a week?"

Bethany looked as if smoke might pour out of her ears.

I shrugged defensively. "Should I even really be talking to you about this?"

"I just want to know what you have planned for this guy so that I can protect my client—who, I should remind you, runs a multibillion-dollar business and cannot be implicated in this sort of circus!"

Hannah tore around the corner at that moment, but she stopped short when she saw her attorney. "Oh, hi."

Bethany put her hands on her hips. "Oh, *hi*, yourself! I've sent you ten texts this week and you haven't responded, and now I know why."

"Sorry." Hannah bit her lip.

Bethany scowled. "I want to know about your source—the 'happy' one. I need to know what the hell is going on around here!"

She tapped her heel, the sound echoing across the hardwood floors.

"My source is good—everything's fine." Hannah's brow furrowed into a deep *v*. "Why are you in the guesthouse? Are they having you interview Carey?"

"Jesus, you're involved in this, too?" Bethany flung up her hands and issued another litany of curses.

We probably *should* have had her interview Carey. Bethany could be little scary, and we hadn't gotten that far with him.

Levi came out of the room then and closed the door behind him, the lines in his face etched deeper from lack of sleep. He looked wary when Bethany turned her scowl his way.

"I'm hoping you have some kind of explanation?" she asked. "The kind that keeps my client out of jail for being a criminal accessory?"

He held up his hands, as if in surrender. "Lauren's not involved in any way—this is my company's deal. She can't be implicated whatsoever."

"This is her *house*," Bethany said. "What were you thinking?"

Levi stalked toward her, the muscles in his jaw clenched. "I was *thinking* that it'd be safer for Lauren and *for everyone* if we didn't let Li Na's little henchmen stalk, murder, or kidnap anyone else for a change. Keep your friends close and your enemies closer, and all."

"Has he actually told you anything useful?" Bethany didn't sound impressed.

Levi examined his knuckles, which were bloody. "Not yet. I'm working on it."

Bethany shook her head.

"Why don't you let us talk to him?" Hannah offered. "He might appreciate a fresh approach—one that doesn't involve beating on him. We might be able to motivate him."

I put myself between her and the doorway. "No way, babe."

Hannah arched an eyebrow. "I didn't ask you, *babe*—I asked your boss."

Levi rubbed his forehead as if he had a headache.

Bethany crossed her arms. "I can only go in there if Levi's my client. Otherwise, I can't protect him from this mess—I need attorney-client privilege for that."

"If you think you can get somewhere, I'd be happy to retain you. Maybe we can discuss it over dinner?" Levi chuckled darkly as Bethany's cheeks flushed.

"I'll get him to talk. Is there a guard in there?"

"Two."

"Then we should be fine." Bethany stalked around him, careful to keep her distance.

Hannah moved to follow, but I blocked her again.

"Back *off*," she said. "This is my company and my family, too, dammit. Don't treat me like a child!"

I didn't want to treat her badly, but I also didn't want her anywhere near harm's way. I took a deep breath, reconciling these competing desires. "Can I at least come in with you?"

Her face softened. "Of course you can."

Levi motioned us toward the door. "I'd come, too, but I'm pretty sure Carey's had enough of me for one night."

"You don't say," Bethany muttered under her breath.

"Can't wait to hear how it goes." Levi smiled at her, largely undeterred. "I'll be waiting right here so you can tell me all about it."

Bethany just shook her head.

Inside the room, Carey appeared worse for wear. His jaw was bruised, and there was a fresh cut over his eyebrow. His hoodie was long gone, replaced by a rumpled, bloodstained T-shirt. He was handcuffed to the leg of a table and sat slumped over it.

I might've imagined it, but he seemed to perk up a little when Hannah and Bethany came into the room.

Bethany noticed it, too. "Don't get too excited. We're not going to hit you, but we're not as nice as Levi."

Carey slumped again. "What do you want? I already told them, I don't know anything about the client. I only know the assignment came from China."

Hannah sat down on the other side of the room, her pretty face scrunching as she examined his wounds. "Would your boss be able to tell us who the client is or confirm any information?"

Carey scoffed. "If my boss felt like it, sure. But being cooperative isn't high on their priority list."

Bethany sat down and crossed her legs. "Is federal prison high on their priority list? Because acting as a proxy for an international business partner and committing crimes for hire constitute federal offenses—the kind that can get you put away for a long time."

Carey tilted his head. "I'm pretty sure my boss is aware of all that. And isn't concerned."

"All they care about is money?" Hannah asked.

He shrugged. "I don't care what they care about. I do my job and that's it. I don't analyze."

"I get it." Bethany adjusted her gold bangle. "You're just a gun for hire—you go in and take care of your assignment, and you're out. You're a pawn."

"I like to think of it as punching the clock, but sure. I'm a pawn. I can't tell you anything because I don't know anything. Like I said, I *don't care*."

"So you don't have any loyalty to your boss, or to your client." Hannah smiled. "Right?"

Carey looked from one woman to the other, clearly confused. "Is this going anywhere? 'Cause otherwise, I have a nap to take before that other guy comes back for my regularly scheduled beating."

"We want you to work for us," Hannah said brightly.

Bethany whipped her head toward her, blonde hair flying. "*That's* where we're going with this?"

Hannah shrugged and turned back to Carey. "I'll triple whatever they're paying you *if* you can find out more information for me. I'll give you plenty of cash so you can bribe sources on an as-needed basis. There'll be more money after that. And I'm *nice*. I won't even let Levi beat you up anymore."

"It was the other guy I was worried about," Carey said. "The one built like a boulder."

Ellis.

"Ah," Hannah said. "I'll take care of it."

"I'd make sure he can actually be useful first," Bethany suggested.

Carey glared at her.

Hannah shrugged. "He'll be useful, or he'll get Ellis'd."

I tried not to whine that she wasn't offering to have him Wes'd. "Are we done here?" I asked instead. I wanted Hannah away from this scumbag.

"We're going to get some details, and Bethany's going to write up a little legal document for me and Carey so he knows this is legitimate. Okay, Bethany?"

Bethany fake-smiled at her. "Great. Just how I want to spend my evening: drafting an agreement between one of my best friends and a low-level assassin with questionable hygiene. Just perfect. I hope you'll testify before the Board of Bar Overseers that the subject matter wasn't illegal, or I'm going to be out of a license."

"I'm not asking him to do anything illegal." Hannah raised an eyebrow. "But if you'd rather go, Levi's waiting outside—"

"Enough," Bethany snapped, opening up her laptop and setting up shop across from Carey. "Let's just get this over with."

* * *

HANNAH

Wes came around the corner and handed me a glass of wine. "Honey?"

"Yes?"

He sank down onto the couch next to me. "What the hell was that about?"

I took a sip. "I'm taking my own advice—throwing money at the problem."

He scrubbed a hand across his face. "Huh?"

"It's something I always used to say to Lauren: 'Throw some money at the problem.' She always tries to do everything herself, but once she got to a certain point in her business, it didn't make sense anymore. Hiring the best talent she could find saved her from spreading herself too thin. I still have to remind her to hire help."

Wes scowled. "Honey, if you think Carey is the best talent out there, I'm pretty sure you're going to be disappointed."

I nodded. "Yeah, he's not that impressive. But he's got the contacts, and he's accessible, and he *certainly* wants my money—so I can motivate him. All I want is for him to keep tabs on his employer and to get me names when I need them. Trust me—it'll all work out."

He had a sip of wine, probably so he didn't have to disagree with me.

"I'm doing the same thing with Biyu," I explained.

"I thought you threatened her."

"I *did*, but then I also told her that the more information she got me, the more I could help her." The idea had come to me after I'd spent too much time feeling terrible for threatening her family. Not all motivation had to be negative, I'd decided. "Her child's going to have a trust fund now."

Wes coughed. "You didn't tell me that."

"I just sort of came up with it." I rubbed his back while he recovered. "The thing is, I made a *lot* of money from my Paragon stock. More than I'd ever thought I'd have in one lifetime. And I don't need all that money. I figured this way, Biyu has a vested interest in helping me. She has a stake in the outcome, and she'll be loyal to me because I'm going to help her, just like she's helping me."

"*Is* she actually helping you?"

"Yes. She's confirmed that Li Na's moving ahead. She's building a prototype of the sensor."

"Your plan's working." Wes grinned.

"So far."

I tried to beat my anxiety back. Each step we took, we got closer to the end. I just didn't know how it was going to turn out.

CHAPTER 23

HANNAH

"It's live on Jiàn's website!" I jumped on the computer in Lauren's office, scrolling to the announcement. My inbox was filled with media alerts. Li Na had published the news about her impending launches to her site, and hundreds of news outlets had picked up the story. "She said they're rolling out two cancer-related technologies. Look, she even goes into some detail about what the new products do."

Lauren read the piece silently, biting her lip the whole time. "She's taking the bait—it's working. My baby sister's a genius!"

My face heated, but not with pleasure. "Not so fast. We have to find out what's happening internally. Li Na's a lot of things, but gullible isn't one of them."

"I think she believes this is all legitimate. She *terrorized* Fiona into selling. Li Na's not expecting to be double-crossed, not after what she did."

I nodded. Lauren had a point about that.

"And it isn't gullible of her to believe Paragon's technology is solid. This is *me* we're talking about—I'm cautious, painstaking in my research. Li Na knows she can trust my work. That's why she keeps stealing it." Lauren laughed without humor.

"I know all that, but the fact that this is moving forward as planned... Is it okay if I'm just waiting for the other shoe to drop?"

"Yeah, it is. Li Na's proven herself worthy of our paranoia, if nothing else." Lauren scrolled back through the story, but I could tell her thoughts were elsewhere.

"I'll get Dave and Leo to hack into Jiàn and look around. Can you touch base with your source to find out what's going on behind the scenes?"

"Of course."

I was headed for my office, composing an email to Biyu in my head, when Lauren caught up to me, almost out of breath. I knew something had been percolating in the vast recesses of her brain.

"One other thing—we need to move *fast*. If Li Na's already working on the prototype, she's going to start testing soon. It could happen as early as next week. We need to stay out in front of her and make sure they're not tipped off that the reporting's faulty. Because if that happens, this all blows up."

"Got it." My stomach tied itself in a knot.

Lauren read the expression on my face and sighed. "No pressure or anything."

I laughed. "Right. None at all."

I dashed off a quick email to Biyu, but with the time difference, I didn't expect to hear back right away. I was wrong. My email notification went off immediately.

Working on the prototype nonstop. The staff has been sleeping in the lab. Please don't contact me again. I won't be in touch for a while.

I sent a note back. *Why not?*

She replied a moment later. *I'm having second thoughts.*

I waited for some further explanation, but that was all she wrote.

I paced my office for the rest of the morning, unsettled and fretting. I didn't know what to do about Biyu. I finally dragged myself down for lunch with Lauren, Brian following close behind. "I miss Wes guarding me," I told him, "and I'm still pissed at you for making fun of me the other day." The fact that he'd mimicked me pleading with Wes stuck in my craw.

Brian frowned. "I said I was sorry."

"Don't make fun of me for getting emotional," I said, getting emotional. My nerves were fraught, close to snapping.

"I was just teasing Wes—which I consider part of my job. For the record, I think it's good that you get emotional. It makes you human."

I shot him a look, perplexed and touched. "Thank you?"

"You're welcome," he said easily. "Does that mean you forgive me?"

"Sure." I refused to hang on to any more grudges at the moment, as I only had time for a particularly mammoth one.

I collapsed into a seat in Lauren's office. "Biyu already emailed me back."

"And?" It was her turn to pick up lunch; she pushed a salad across her desk to me.

I ignored it. "*And* she said they were working around the clock on the prototype. She also said she wouldn't be in touch for a while, because she's having second thoughts about our arrangement."

Lauren blew out a deep breath. "I'm sorry to hear that."

"Not as sorry as I am." I grabbed the salad and angrily pushed it around with my fork, as if all this were the bib lettuce's fault. "I don't know what I can do for her."

"Just let it lie for now," Lauren suggested. "Maybe she's being paranoid?"

I frowned. "I wouldn't blame her. I'd be paranoid if I worked for that tyrant."

The phone buzzed with a call from Stephanie, Lauren's assistant. "It's Leo." She patched him through.

"I'd love some good news." Lauren waited.

"It's sort of good, in a twisted way. The Protocol files hit Jiàn's servers. We're ready to set the virus on it, when you give the word."

Lauren didn't hesitate. "Do it now. I'd rather get to the files before the lab workers have a chance to thoroughly examine them—this way, they'll be seeing the technology fresh. They won't have anything to compare them to. But Fiona will still have her copy of the intact files from the initial transmission, so she'll appear innocent—there's no way she can be blamed for this."

"We're on it." Leo hung up without saying anything further.

I smiled at my sister, impressed. "I have to say, you're pretty good at this reverse-hacking thing."

She smiled wanly. "I learned from the best—Li Na herself. Now, can you call Fiona to update her about all this? I'm swamped this afternoon."

I gave up on my salad and stood. "Of course. I'll call her now."

"Don't you want your lunch?" Lauren called.

"I've officially lost my appetite." I hustled down the hall before she could scold me.

I'd only spoken to Fiona a couple of times since the day we'd gone to Mado; traumatized by the incident, she'd pulled Katie and Quinn from school. She'd been busy trying to work from home while coordinating tutors for the girls. She had stopped leaving the house, having groceries delivered and conducting meetings via Skype from her living room.

Ellis had told Wes that the drama of that day had gotten to her—her brief glimpse of feeling safe after Jim's shooting had passed. Now Fiona was pulling out all the stops to protect her daughters.

She answered on the first ring. "Hey." Her voice was scratchy, as if she was coming down with something or she hadn't slept.

"Are you okay?" I asked.

She sighed. "The police and Agent Marks from the FBI just left. They don't have any leads on Jim's shooter, and I'm just…I don't know. At my wit's end."

Carey, my hired traitor, was looking into this for me. He'd promised to canvass his network of hired guns to find out who was responsible for killing Jim Pace. I hadn't mentioned it to Fiona—I didn't want to get her hopes up about finding the attacker.

"I'm so sorry," I said instead.

"I know. It's very frustrating." She paused for a beat. "What's going on over there? The license deal went through yesterday—I still can't believe I did it, that I sold to that…murderer. I figured there would be news."

"Leo confirmed that the files were uploaded to Jiàn's servers today. They're beginning the reverse-hack."

Fiona exhaled shakily. "I don't know about this anymore. I don't know if this is the answer."

"I don't know, either." I traced a pattern on my desk with my finger, wishing things were different, easier. "I don't think there's a rational, direct way to deal with someone like Li Na. I think the best we can hope for is some sort of justice."

"Justice. Huh." Fiona sounded as if she might be crying, and I crumbled inside. "I don't know if anything like that's going to happen."

I didn't, either. "That's not going to stop me from trying."

"We need to talk about that. About you. I've been thinking about you." She blew her nose, seeming to collect herself.

"What do you mean?"

"You've taken on a lot of the responsibility for dealing with Li Na. You need to be clear about why you're doing this." Fiona perked up at the topic. Generous, direct, and analytical, she was at her best in mentor mode—the main reason her book had been an international bestseller.

She cleared her throat, no longer crying, and continued. "One of the things I always ask a new hire is, 'Why do you want to be here? What's in it for you?' Because the personal informs the professional. You have to be passionate about your choices for it to really sync, for you to be fully committed. That concept applies here."

I closed my eyes, images running through my head: the guard leering at me, Wes going down hard after getting shot, Fiona's stricken face at the funeral. "I feel pretty passionate about taking Li Na down."

"I know you do—but what's the reason? And I mean the real reason: what's in it for *you*?"

I thought of Wes holding me, feeling safe in his arms. "The future. I need a future without Li Na terrorizing the people I love."

"Well…then you'll probably be successful, or at least go down fighting," Fiona said. "I just hoped this wasn't about revenge for you or proving yourself. You don't need either."

But of course, I'd like both. I thought about that for a second—was it true? Maybe, but just as I couldn't fathom Li Na being solely motivated by "face," I didn't believe myself capable of hurting others just for revenge. I wasn't wired that way. "It's not about that. It's about my family."

"In the end, that's all that matters."

I winced. Fiona had lost the person who mattered most to her.

"Revenge is lovely in theory, but in practice? There aren't enough hours in my lifetime to get back at Li Na. And nothing can undo what she's done."

"You're right about that." Her voice was gravelly.

"Are Katie and Quinn okay? Ellis said you pulled them from school."

"I was too worried after we were followed. The girls had security at the academy, but I'd rather have them home where I know we're protected. It's too much of a risk right now. And I'm staying right here with them—me, my mom, the girls, and a dozen security guards. It's quite the setup."

She laughed, but it sounded brittle. "What's going on with him, anyway—the man who was following us? Ellis won't tell me anything. He says it's safer if I don't know."

"Ellis is smart." His rabid protection of Fiona touched me. I tapped my pen against the desk, wondering if I could tell her anything without putting her in harm's way.

But the risk was too great. "I don't know what happened to the guy. Wes wants me out of the loop, too."

Actually, the guy—Carey—had been set free on my direct order. I was paying his rent, I'd leased him a new car, and he was on an urgent fact-finding mission for me. If he delivered, I was giving him a rather large lump-sum payment, the size of which had Wes reeling.

But I considered it proper motivation.

"Well, keep me posted on the Shenzhen situation. I know Li Na made an announcement today, even if she didn't name names. I don't expect her to disclose the Protocol deal until she has government confirmation of all the necessary approvals."

"Lauren said that this is going to move quickly. We have to keep an eye on things."

Fiona exhaled deeply. "What's done is done. Let's just hope this works."

I stared out the window, still nervously tapping. Most of this had been my idea. If we failed, it was on me. "We should probably come up with a Plan B."

"I think we're living Plan B—surrounded by security, our respective companies' innovation stifled, scared of our own shadows. I like Plan A better."

I sighed. "I like it better, too. If it works."

* * *

WES

"If you think Biyu's in danger, we need to do something."

I lifted a dumbbell while I did a squat and cursed—getting back into shape was a bitch, even without my evil physical therapist around.

Hannah was in a fresh hell all her own, doing a sit-up that involved lifting her legs while simultaneously hoisting a dumbbell against her chest. "I don't know what I can do for her. I don't even know what the problem is."

"Is she still going into work? Have you checked her bank account—has she withdrawn money?"

"She seems to be maintaining her routine. Leo checked on her." Hannah pushed a sweaty lock of hair off her forehead. "It looks like she bought groceries last night, she paid the daycare this morning, went to a takeout place for lunch."

"So she's in Shenzhen, and she's still at Jiàn. But she doesn't want to talk to you."

Hannah frowned. "And I don't know why. She told me not to contact her, but I need to know the status of the prototype."

"Give her a day or two. Things could be really intense, especially if Li Na's overseeing the crazy production schedule. It could be an all-hands-on-deck situation." I did another squat and forced my face to remain neutral so Hannah couldn't see I that was actually about to die.

She dropped the barbell with a groan and sat up. "Can you ask Ellis to reach out to one of his contacts? I'd love it if someone could put eyes on Biyu, or maybe get her a message that's not attached to a hackable account."

"He was never a hundred percent that he'd be able to reach anybody," I reminded her.

"I know it's a long shot. But will you ask? I'm going crazy because I don't know what's happening—I don't know if she's in danger."

I set my own barbell down, grateful that I had a valid excuse to quit. "I'll see if he wants to grab a quick dinner, and I'll ask him about it. Okay?"

"Thank you for everything that you do. I'll never be able to say it enough."

She smiled at me, stop-you-in-your-tracks gorgeous even as she wiped the sweat from her forehead.

"Sure you will," I growled, leaning down for a sweaty but still lingering kiss.

Hannah swatted me, grinning as we broke apart. "You can earn extra credit with me later—after you see Ellis and, more importantly, after you *take a shower.*"

* * *

After what had happened with Carey, my brother refused to leave Fiona's house, so I grabbed takeout and a six-pack and brought them over. He ushered me into the kitchen; we could hear Fiona on a conference call in her study.

"Don't you *ever* take a day off?"

He put a plate in front of me and scowled. "With everything that's been going on, no."

"Don't you need to go home to change? Take a shower? Hit the gym?"

Ellis bit into the burger and didn't answer until he'd finished chewing. "Don't have to. I have everything I need here."

"So you're basically living here."

He shrugged and kept eating.

"Listen, Hannah needs a favor."

"Hannah, or you?"

"Hannah." He wouldn't do it for me.

"Fine. What does she need?"

"Her contact in Shenzhen's dropped out. She said she can't talk for a while. Hannah just wants to confirm that she's okay, and also maybe get a message to her."

"Sounds like she's not interested in getting a message." He grabbed a handful of my sweet potato fries and ate them before I could protest.

I sighed—he was right. "Do you have someone who could check on her? Shenzhen's not far from Hong Kong."

Ellis gave me a look. "I know where it is, little brother."

"Do you know anybody who can do it *now*? We'll pay them, make it worth their while."

"Like our other buddy—the one from the parking lot?" Ellis kept his voice low, but he sounded pissed. He didn't approve of the fact that Carey, aka Mr. Gray Hoodie, was free and on our payroll.

I took a swig of beer. "That was Hannah's idea, and it was a pretty good one. She's paying him to find out information that we couldn't get otherwise. The police and the FBI have been completely useless."

My brother leaned closer, glowering. "If I see that dude's face again, I'm going to break it."

"Can you just give me an answer about Shenzhen?"

"The answer is maybe. I'll let you know."

I wanted to ask when, but Fiona came in.

"Hey, Wes. I didn't know you were here. Sorry to interrupt." She bustled around in the pantry, finally retrieving a bag of organic fish crackers. "The girls want a snack. Can I get you two anything?"

"No, but thank you."

Ellis didn't say anything. He stared in her direction after she left the room.

"Everything okay?" I asked.

He grabbed his beer. "Yeah—she's just been through a lot. So have the girls. I want to make this go away so they can move on."

I watched him. Was that...*concern* playing out on my brother's face?

"What?" His tone was sharp.

"It's nothing." With my brother, less was always more, and nothing was best. "So...can you help me? And by me, I mean Hannah."

"I'll help. If it gets rid of Zhao, I'm in."

Chapter 24

HANNAH

"Have you heard anything from Biyu?" Wes asked me.

"No. Have you heard anything from Ellis?"

He shook his head. "He reached out to his friend, but I don't know anything else."

"Keep me posted, okay?" I leaned down and gave him a quick kiss. "I have to get to the office."

"Do you want me to come with you today instead of Brian?"

I put a hand on my hip. "Levi told me he's got you busy transcribing field notes and writing reports. Which I think is *perfect*, seeing as you're still on *restricted duty*."

Wes grimaced. "Gee, thanks. I'd rather gouge my eye out with a pencil than do more paperwork, but if *you* think it's a good idea…"

"Oh, honey, I'm sorry."

But even though I'd vowed to be supportive, I wasn't sorry in the slightest. The longer Wes stayed on restricted duty, the longer he was safe. I patted his broad shoulder, which felt firm beneath my touch—he wouldn't be deskbound much longer.

"Can you leave work early today? There's a house I want to take a look at."

I shook my head. "I don't think so—I have a ton of calls to make. Maybe we can grab dinner after, and then you can tell me all about it?"

"Sounds good." He reached up and kissed me, making my body ache for him. When he pulled back, I realized I still felt achy. My head thudded.

Wes narrowed his eyes. "You okay?"

"Yeah, I just need to drink some water. I'll see you later. Love you."

When I got to the office, I poured myself a large glass of water and settled at my desk. I relaxed as I cleaned out my email inbox, getting it back to zero new messages, right where I liked it. Still, I had a lot of work to do. The international business journals were jockeying around me, asking for an exclusive on the story I'd promised. I'd decided to commit to *The Wall Street Journal*—they were prestigious, had a huge readership, and were distinctly American—all the better to annoy Li Na.

I sent an email to my friend who worked there, Calvin, telling him about my decision to give him the exclusive.

And then I ran into my bathroom and promptly threw up.

What the hell? I sat on the bathroom floor, reeling, but the nausea passed quickly.

By the time I got back to my desk, I was shaking. Part of me worried I was about to have another panic attack or that I was coming down with a stomach bug. But after a minute, I realized I didn't have the chills—I was just starving. I smacked my head. I'd forgotten to eat breakfast, and when I thought back further, I realized I hadn't been eating my normal load over the past few days. I'd been too upset about Biyu. No wonder I felt like crap.

I hustled to the cafeteria where I got my usual, a vanilla protein shake and a salad with roasted beets and goat cheese. Back in my office, I arranged my food and had a big slug of my shake. My mouth immediately puckered—it tasted sour. I put the lid on it, setting it aside in disgust. I bent to have a bite of my salad, but the smell of the marinated beets was too pungent. Usually I loved them, but today, *ugh*. Maybe I *was* coming down with a stomach bug?

But at the thought of my stomach, it howled with hunger.

All of a sudden, I knew what I wanted. Vegetable lo mein, the greasy kind, from the Chinese takeout place on Sixth Street. I pulled up the menu and called them, then called Brian and whined until he agreed to drive me there.

Who cared that is was only ten thirty in the morning?

* * *

"Calvin Jakes is on line one for you," my assistant said.

"Put him through."

"Hey, Hannah."

Calvin's voice was bright and warm. I easily conjured the image of my friend from Stanford who had strawberry-blond hair, a smattering of freckles, and a charming smile—all of which probably helped him disarm his interviews subjects and scoop the best stories.

"Hi! It's so nice to hear your voice." *Too bad it's under such insane circumstances.* I kept the thought to myself and arranged my crispy spring rolls in a neat line, so I could eat them in order of appearance as soon as I got off the phone.

"I know, right? I was psyched to get your message. I was worried you were going to give the exclusive to the *Financial Times*."

"I thought about it…" I absently played with the spring rolls.

"You haven't changed your mind, have you?"

I snapped to attention. "Not at all. I want to give the exclusive to you, but you need to get your editors to understand—this is a big story. When the time comes, you're going to need space. I want this on the front page, and I need you to commit to that."

"The front page is yours."

"Great. I appreciate it, and I'm happy we're working together."

"Me too, me too." Calvin paused for a second. "But can't you tell me *anything* about the details of this story? Like: who it involves? What it's about?"

"I can't tell you anything more than it involves major players from Silicon Valley and also from China. Trust me, this news is going to blow the doors off the biotech world."

"Does this have anything to do with what happened to you? The kidnapping?"

I sat up straight, no longer playing with my food. "How did you know about that?"

"People talk. Some of our classmates who work in tech heard about it, and they told me you'd been kidnapped. What happened?"

"I don't want to talk about that." My voice came out harsher than I intended. "And the story's in no way related, so let it go, okay? Or bye-bye exclusive."

"Don't say bye-bye—you know I want this story. I wasn't trying to make you upset, I swear. Just trying to dig a little deeper. You're being so mysterious and all."

I sighed. "Would it make you feel better if I told you I was doing it for a good reason?"

"Sure—as long as you let me in on what the reason is someday soon. And let me write about it."

* * *

WES

Ellis had been ordered to take a day off, so I asked him to meet me at the house I'd been eyeing. I texted him the address, then headed over to meet with the realtor.

He showed up just as the broker was leaving. He let out a low whistle as he stood in the driveway, looking up at the large home, which boasted skylights, an elegant stone driveway, and a three-car garage. He clapped me on the back. "This place is something else. Makes our old house look like a shack."

I squinted at the lawn, feeling proud but also a little embarrassed by the house's grand appearance. "Mom and Dad would have a fit if they knew the list price."

Our parents were hardy, Midwestern middle-class stock. They had a lot of money from their respective families, but you would never know it by how they lived—modest, split-level home, pre-owned cars, and dinner made in the Crock-Pot, not some trendy restaurant like Mado.

"They'd be proud of you, and they'd want you to have it, for you and Hannah." Ellis gave me the side-eye. "Speaking of Hannah, did you ask her to move in with you yet?"

I looked down at my shoes, which suddenly needed inspecting. "Not yet."

"C'mon, bro. You don't make a woman like that wait."

Now I gave *him* the side-eye—since when did he give me relationship advice? "What's going on with you?"

He frowned. "I'm your big brother. I'm just trying to help."

I waved him off. "Yeah, I know that. But I mean, what's going *on* with you?"

Ellis looked stymied. "I came here to tell you about my contact, who's now in Shenzhen on *your* dime."

That wasn't what I meant, but I let him continue.

"He's been doing surveillance on Biyu—she's fine, her son is fine, she's just going to work and going home, sticking to her normal routine." He shrugged. "He's going to watch her for the next few days, but I warned him to stay away from Jiàn Innovations. He knows Li Na by reputation. He understands he has to be careful."

"Good. Thank you. Do you think he'll be comfortable approaching Biyu when the time comes?"

"Maybe," Ellis said.

"Explain that we'll make it worth his while."

"Fine. What's the message for Biyu?"

I shrugged. "That if she doesn't make contact soon, not only is the deal off, but that she should be worried."

Ellis raised an eyebrow. "I take it that message is from you, not Hannah."

"She's ready to play hardball. Speaking of Hannah, I have to get going. I'm meeting her for dinner. Want to join us?"

He shrugged. "I guess so."

"Who made you take the day off—Fiona or Levi?"

He shrugged again. "Both."

"Why do you look so miserable?"

Ellis grunted. "I don't do days off. I live in a climate-controlled mansion by myself—what the hell am I supposed to do all day? By the way, the cleaning service came by. They said you paid them?"

"I figured you didn't have time to clean toilets since you've been working nonstop."

"Uh, thanks?"

I grimaced. "Uh, you're welcome?"

"I don't mean to be ungrateful. I just…I guess I don't know what to do with myself. In the desert, if we had time off, we played cards and cleaned the barracks." He frowned. "Everything's already clean, here. It's shiny and perfect and everybody drives a Range Rover. It's frickin' la-la land."

"So you'd rather be at work."

He ran his hands over his buzz cut. "Fuck *yeah*, I'd rather be at work. At least I'm doing something."

"And things with Fiona are fine?"

He turned and leveled me with a blazing glare. "Why the hell do you keep asking me that?"

"I don't."

He held the glare.

"You seem attached," I said finally.

"I don't want her to die on my watch. *Okay?*" His voice blistered.

"Okay. Sheesh."

He stalked toward his car—the Range Rover Levi had given him for company use.

"Are you still coming to dinner?"

He mumbled something under his breath as he peeled out of the driveway. It sounded suspiciously like *Fuck no*.

I sighed. I should've known better. With Ellis, less was more, and saying nothing was always best.

Chapter 25

HANNAH

Ellis's contact worked faster than I could have wished for—Biyu emailed me the next evening.

Don't have that man come near me again! You're putting me in danger!

I took a deep breath and wrote back immediately.

Let's talk via Skype. We have a lot to go through—I'm not done with you yet.

I sent her my account link and pulled up the site, hoping she'd cooperate.

Biyu's pretty face, twisted into a scowl, appeared on my monitor moments later. I could see the bare walls of her drab-looking apartment in the background. "I don't want to talk for long. My son's sleeping—I don't want to disturb him. And I don't want that man coming around again!"

"Fine." I licked my lips. "But you've put yourself in this position by not keeping your promise to me. I need an update."

"And I need money, lots of it, if you want me to do this."

"I set up the trust for your son, and I linked it to another account that you can pull cash from." I gave her the bank information. "You can look it up—I just made another deposit."

Biyu tapped away on a tablet until she found what she was looking for. Her eyes got wide when she looked at the accounts—I'd been generous. "I see it. Thank you."

"You're welcome. Now tell me what I need to know."

She sighed, tucking her hair behind her ear. "The prototype's complete. We begin testing tomorrow."

"That was fast."

Biyu nodded. "Li Na had the team sleep on site all week. No one on the technical team's left the premises, except for a celebratory dinner."

"You're already celebrating? Did you go to the dinner?"

"Yes. Even I was invited." A note of pride crept into her voice. "And we're not celebrating about the releases yet—Li Na was celebrating *us*. Jiàn's employees. She wants us all to know she appreciates the sacrifices we're making."

Concerned and somewhat appalled by her reverential tone, I snorted. "Oh, Li Na knows all about making sacrifices, all right—making *other people sacrifice for what she wants*."

Biyu's chin rose stubbornly. "I don't know if I can talk to you anymore, even with all that money. You can say what you want about Li Na, but she's doing amazing things for my country."

"She stole my sister's technology, and that's the least of it. She's done terrible things, Biyu—criminal things. Don't underestimate her—and don't underestimate what she could do to you."

"I don't. But you shouldn't underestimate her, either—do you know that this is the first job I've been able to find since I graduated from university? Jiàn is one of the few companies that's actively recruiting right now. The fact that Li Na's trying to bring jobs and prestige to Shenzhen is huge for us. I don't know that what you're offering is better than what she can give me: a job with a future."

I shook my head. "There isn't a future with Jiàn. She's built her company with lies and stolen intellectual property. She won't be able to sustain this pace forever, and I'm going to take her down. You need to get out. Take the money I offered you—there's more where that came from, a lot more. And when the time comes, I'll make sure you land on your feet. But you have to help me. I need to know exactly what's going on with the production and what's happening next."

We stared at each other for a beat.

"She's not the savior you think she is."

Biyu frowned. "Why should I trust *you*?"

"You don't have to trust me. You just have to choose my money over hers, and I'm offering more. Can you do that?" I held my breath, hoping that this was actually going to pay off.

After a minute, Biyu sighed. "I don't feel good about it, but yes, I can do that."

"I don't feel good about it, either, but still—great. I'm glad to hear it. Now please tell me where Li Na's at with the sensor."

* * *

Biyu and I stayed in frequent contact. I made sure that Leo monitored all her accounts for signs of spying or hacking, but things appeared calm.

She remained undetected. I'd chosen our source wisely—her position within Jiàn was entry-level, and it kept her in a different ecosphere than Li Na. Thank God.

Leo also confirmed that the reverse-hack of the Protocol files had taken effect—the specs had subtly been rewritten. The therapy would appear to be intact, but it wouldn't function the same as the one tested here in Silicon Valley—and it wouldn't work. But the push through the Chinese regulatory approval process wouldn't flag the issue: they weren't taking the time to fully conduct clinical trials, relying instead on the successful American trial results. They were fast-tracking the therapy without double-checking that the Chinese version perfectly emulated the American results.

People could get sick from this therapy. And as much as I wanted to ruin Li Na, I couldn't let it go that far—I had to stop the therapy before it went to market.

I had a similar issue with the sensor. On a fast-track through the approval process, it wouldn't be subjected to extensive clinical trials. The Chinese government was again relying on the pending approvals of the American government.

The pending approvals which were fakes.

I had to stop the sensor before it went to market. Its false positives would mislead patients and potentially harm them. But the timing had to be perfect. In order to maximize her shame, I needed Li Na to get as far as a formal announcement before I broke the news of the stolen and defective technology.

That wasn't my only logistical concern. I needed proof. I needed more than just a story.

On an atypical night, we were all home from work at a decent hour. Gabe had started a fire in the fire pit, and we were outdoors enjoying the cool weather and the stars. I caught Gabe, Lauren, and Wes up on the latest developments in my scheme, including all the news outlets I'd lined up to run the story as soon as *The Wall Street Journal* broke the story.

"So…it's working out?" Gabe stoked the fire, watching the sparks fly.

"So far, so good." But I couldn't shake the feeling that things were running too smoothly, that the calm surrounding the situation was about to morph into a storm that would blow up directly in my face.

"You're being too humble." Lauren beamed at me. "You've done an amazing job coordinating this whole thing. Li Na's done exactly what you thought she would—grab for the brass ring without being meticulous about the results. That's basically her trademark move."

"I know…but Biyu sees a different side to her. We know she's a murderer and a thief, but her employees are loyal to her. Biyu said Li Na was devoted to her employees, that she took them out for a special dinner to say thank you for all the hours they've been putting in."

Gabe turned from the fire. "Listen—I'm sure she inspires others. She's impressive, and God knows she's committed to her company. But what she's doing isn't sustainable. Jiàn's only legitimately produced products are fish food in a sea of sharks, and she knows it. She can't build an empire on what she's accomplished, and she can't sustain an empire if all she's truly excellent at is identifying megahit technology and misappropriating it. She's going to run out of road with this eventually. Don't doubt yourself—it might as well be now, and it might as well be us who take her down. Because otherwise, more people are going to get hurt."

He grinned at me. "By the way, do you want some Chardonnay? It's organic and locally sourced, just for you."

"Um, no thanks."

The three of them blinked at me. I rarely said no to a glass of wine after work.

"My stomach's been sort of a mess lately," I admitted. "Stress."

Wes shook his head. "You need to take it easy, baby. I'm making you take a vacation after this."

I laughed softly. "I'll settle for sleeping in on a Saturday."

"I can arrange that." Wes grinned, looking pleased with himself. "Do you want to get going to bed?"

I yawned.

"I guess that's my answer." Wes stood and held his hand out for me.

We said good night to Lauren and Gabe, and Wes wrapped his arm protectively around me as we headed to our bedroom. "I'd pick you up and carry you, but I know you'd just yell at me."

I yawned again. "You're right about that."

"Are you sick, baby? Or just run-down?"

"I think it's just stress, honestly. Which can totally suppress your immune system." Another helpful thing I'd learned from *Grey's Anatomy*.

"Ah. Make sure you drink a green smoothie tomorrow."

I scowled at him. "I will. You can stop making fun of me now."

We took turns brushing our teeth and putting our pajamas on. I sat up and arranged myself sexily on the bed as I waited for Wes, but unfortunately, I couldn't keep my eyes open.

"Babe."

I woke up to Wes tucking me in. "Hi."

He kissed my forehead. "Hi."

I reached up and wrapped my arms around his neck. "I love you."

He grinned down at me. "I love you, too." But instead of coming close for a deep kiss, he wound his arms around me and pulled me against his chest. "Shh, go back to sleep. I got you."

I nestled against his big body. "I thought we were going to do our homework."

Dr. Kathy hadn't given us any, but I'd begun to enjoy bragging about our sex life during therapy.

"Tomorrow. Tonight, I can tell my baby needs to sleep."

"Okay." It came out mumbled, because even as the word left my lips, I was drifting off.

I woke up to the sun streaming through the windows. I looked at the clock and sat up with a start. "Wes! Why'd you let me sleep so late!"

I squinted at the time—could that be right? I'd slept ten hours.

He stuck his head out of the bathroom, shaving cream covering half his face. "You didn't budge all night—no nightmares *again*. I think you're finally past them. Your body's probably resting from all the drama. You just need to catch up on your sleep."

I hustled out of bed. "I need to catch up on my work!"

I bolted past him, stripping out of my pajamas and throwing them on the floor, turning the shower knob on forcefully. I *hated* being late for work. If I didn't wash my hair, I might be able to get out of here in time…

Wes finished shaving, then stuck his head in the shower. "Is there room for me in there?"

"No," I said, grumpily applying shower gel to myself.

He slid in anyway, and I tried not to ogle his enormous, chiseled body. *Damn* but that evil Ashley did nice work.

He caught me eyeing his chest appreciatively and grinned. "Busted."

I started to rinse off. "Am not."

He poked me—I looked down and saw it had been with his huge erection that seemed to be *reaching* for me across the shower stall.

I fake-frowned at him. "Busted."

He poked me again. "I'm a repeat offender. I'm not ashamed to admit it."

I shivered a little, my thighs immediately trembling. *Oh, no you don't*, I warned myself. *Must. Get. To. Work.*

I finished rinsing as Wes eyed me like I was the last juicy rib eye on earth. My heart thudded, rolling over inside my chest as I felt the familiar heat unfurl between us. He reached out, taking my nipple between his fingers. It beaded instantly. I felt moisture that had nothing to do with the shower pool between my legs, and my breath started coming in hot little pants. My body loved Wes, too, and it reacted immediately, opening up for him, eagerly grasping for him, completely out of my control. My body loved the way Wes made it feel, with his tender caresses and his *very*, very large penis.

My body didn't care if I was late for work. My body just wanted to ride that thing.

He kissed me again, tongue roaming.

I guessed I didn't care, either—my email inbox wasn't going anywhere.

And I wanted to ride that thing, too.

I reached for him, leaning up to crush my lips against his. He sank his hands into my hair and positioned me so the hot water ran down my back. I no longer cared that my hair was getting wet. His tongue lashed against mine. Every time we kissed, I had this feeling: an unbearable ache, a longing for him to be inside me.

He ran his fingers over my jawline and put his forehead to mine. "I love you so much, it hurts."

I smiled even as tears sprang to my eyes. I kissed him again, enjoying the sharp pang of all the feelings I had for him. "I love you, too. Now, show me how you feel."

I leaned back against the tiled wall and lifted one of my legs slightly, opening my body up for his. I took his long, hard length in my hand and massaged it, playing with the sensitive tip. I rolled it between my fingers until his head lolled back and he moaned, moving against my palm, lost in how good it felt. When his eyes opened back up, he lazily and expertly put his thumb against my clit, circling it until my actions mirrored his—moaning and moving against his hand, my body begging him to enter me.

Please. Fill me up. I grabbed his ass and pulled him closer, my kisses growing wild. I put his tip against the entrance of my sex, and he notched himself inside me.

He flexed his hips—pure power rolled off him, and I dug my nails into his ass, moving him in deeper. He gave me what I wanted, pumping his hips again so his whole shaft was inside me, stretching me, making me shake against him as he stroked my core.

He thrust into me, and I saw white. He was all the way in, his thick girth filling me like only he could. Our bodies felt made for each other, two interlocking pieces designed to end up together. Lost in the moment, I wrapped my legs around his waist, and he lifted me up, pumping into me hard and fierce. I bounced up and down as I rode him, his penis deep inside me, caressing the place only he could reach.

I saw stars as I came, hard, screaming his name.

Wes's orgasm chased mine. He thrust into me, again and again, his guttural groan turning to a laugh as he finished.

He set me down gently, and I clung to him, shaking.

He kissed me deeply, but I still shuddered when he pulled out, feeling bereft.

"I shouldn't have let you pick me up like that." My cheeks heated in shame.

He tapped my chin so I looked up at him. "I could totally handle it. Want to do that again so I can prove it to you?"

My legs were jelly. "In a perfect world, yes. In this one, I don't think I can handle it." I smiled at him weakly.

He grinned. "I'm just bluffing. I couldn't do that again right now. Maybe ten minutes from now, but that might be wishful thinking."

We both giggled, and I nestled against his chest, the warm water still spraying us. "I love you."

"I love you more, baby. Now get going. The world needs conquering, and you're just the high-powered female executive to do it."

I pulled back, snapping back to reality. "That reminds me."

He was instantly on alert. "Oh boy. What?"

"I need another favor from Ellis."

Wes frowned. "Do you mind asking him yourself? I think I'm on his bad list."

"Why?"

"I kept asking him about Fiona."

I studied his face. "Why'd you do that?"

He shrugged, looking uncomfortable. "I don't know. He just seems…invested."

"Maybe he's just throwing himself into his work."

He looked unconvinced. "Maybe. But you think you can call him this time? You're his favorite."

I rolled my eyes as I turned off the water. "We'll see about that. You don't know what I need to ask him."

Wes raised his eyebrows, questioning, as he toweled himself off.

"And trust me, you don't *want* to know."

"Tell me when the afterglow's faded. I can handle it."

I sighed. "I know you can."

The question was, could I?

Chapter 26

HANNAH

"What if she can't get the samples to him?" Ellis paced my office, looking uneasy—probably because Fiona was locked in a meeting with Lauren and he couldn't see her, and also because of what I'd asked him for.

"She will. She promised."

Biyu *hadn't* promised, exactly, but she'd said she would try.

She wanted to get the samples. I believed that. In addition to the trust fund, I'd offered her plane tickets to California and a fresh start here for her and her son, which included a new car, a condominium, and a position at Paragon—*if* she could deliver.

I hadn't shared the parameters of my offer with Wes. A good, conservative Midwestern boy, he thought I was being a little too extravagant of late.

He might be right, but I needed those samples, dammit. I needed evidence that the claims I was about to make against Li Na Zhao were real. So I'd charged Biyu with the task of stealing lab results for both the gene therapy and the sensor. We could run the labs at Paragon, and then we'd have the proof we needed to show that Jiàn's technology was faulty.

I had to document the process every step of the way, so I'd invited Calvin and a *Wall Street Journal* photographer to join me in Silicon Valley. They would organize and catalog all the evidence, and then we'd reveal the entire story in a front page exclusive.

I paced, waiting for Ellis to say something. Anything.

"I don't think he's going to like being an international courier of corporate-espionage-inspired stolen goods, but he'll do it if the price is right."

I nodded fervently. "The price is right. Whatever he wants, I'll do it."

"Okay." Ellis didn't look like he really thought it was okay.

I continued to pace, not letting myself consider that he might be right.

* * *

"I have a Mr. Carey for you on line two," my assistant said.

"Send him through." I waited until the line clicked over. "It's *Mr.* Carey now?"

"It's just Carey." As usual, my informant sounded humorless and slightly pissed.

"What's going on?"

"I have those names you wanted."

"Great."

He'd been collecting the names of all the independent contractors who'd worked for Li Na over the past year. I wanted to assemble the list for the FBI as further proof of what Li Na had been up to.

"What about the other name we discussed?" I held my breath, hoping he'd been able to find out who was responsible for Jim Pace's death.

"I have the information you're looking for."

"But?"

"*But* it's going to cost you." Carey sounded pleased with himself, and I sincerely wished he had a higher moral fiber.

But I wanted the information. *Bad.* Bad enough to keep Carey in a nice condo and the muscle cars he seemed to prefer. "I'm prepared for that. So, Carey…let's make a deal."

***

It's done, Biyu wrote. *I put the packages into the locker at the airport like you said.*

Did anyone find out? I wrote back, palms sweating.

I don't know, but I'm not going back there to check. The lab has security cameras. See you on the other side, she wrote.

I was going to have to explain an awful lot to Wesley when I picked Biyu and her son up at the airport.

If they made it to the airport.

I paced my office, waiting to hear anything. There was no other news, and I knew I had to wait until Ellis's contact landed on American soil to begin my campaign in earnest.

So for now, the phone was my only weapon. Like any good publicity director, I yielded it expertly. I pulled up my list and started dialing my media contacts, getting everyone buzzing about the news about to break.

Today, I stoked the fire.

Tomorrow, I watched Li Na burn.

***

"He's here. I have the samples. I'll send them to the lab with Levi."

"Thank you, Ellis." I sank down into my chair, relieved.

"You're welcome. Try to stay out of trouble long enough to finish this thing, okay?"

I could hear the grin in his voice.

"Okay."

I immediately called Calvin after I hung up with Ellis. "The samples are on their way. We're getting started this afternoon."

Calvin and the photographer were staying at an Airbnb in town.

"We'll be there. I can't wait to find out what the hell these are samples of—they better be good!"

"They are."

"I know. I can tell you're nervous—and you wouldn't be nervous if this wasn't a big deal. See you in a few."

I could hear the grin in his voice, too.

Nerves thrumming with adrenaline, I prepared a list of all the steps I needed to take over the next twenty-four hours. By the time Levi arrived with the stolen samples, I was ready to move forward into my future, one that didn't involve Li Na Zhao.

* * *

Lauren herself oversaw the testing of the Jiàn Innovations samples. "I'm writing a formal report, one we can file with the Chinese government—they need to know about this, too. They need to be more careful."

While we waited for her to finish the report, Calvin interviewed me. I told him everything, from the beginning—how Li Na tried to steal the patch, what had happened to Clive Warren, everything. His mouth hung open a lot of the time.

I told him about being kidnapped. I told him about Wes. I told him about Jim Pace and Protocol Therapeutics.

After we finished our interview and Lauren completed the report, Calvin took his copy and went to file his story. That was when I called Agent Marks from the FBI, giving him the list of names Carey had provided me with.

I gave him the name of the man who shot Jim Pace.

I didn't give him Carey's name, which Bethany was having an absolute fit about, but a deal was a deal.

"Even if that makes you an accessory?" Bethany spluttered.

I sighed. "I guess so."

She stalked out of my office, high heels clicking angrily down the hall.

Hours later, Calvin called me. "The story's about to go live." Now *he* sounded nervous. "Be prepared for the onslaught."

Levi had quadrupled security, but the FBI was busy rounding up Li Na's henchmen. So maybe we were safe. She didn't have many warm bodies left to hire.

I paced my office until I gave up and kept hitting the refresh button. Finally, I saw the headline: *Chinese CEO Kills for Silicon Valley Biotechnology.* The subtitle read: *Defective, Stolen Products Approved by Chinese Government.* I scanned the rest of the article, which named Li Na Zhao and discussed at length how the stolen technology was just days away from being sold to patients.

A minute later, my phone started ringing.

But before I answered, I gave myself one brief moment to gloat. *You did it.*

Smiling, I answered the phone.

* * *

LI NA

Like most things, I knew before anyone else. As per my normal routine, I woke at four a.m., logged onto my laptop, and read all the day's headlines and industry news.

I read all the day's headlines and industry news *about me and my company.*

Chinese CEO Kills. This was bad enough.

Defective Products Approved by Chinese Government. But this one undid me.

I could barely face my own disgrace. But my country, my people… We'd been caught looking the fool in front of the whole world.

Rage pulsed through me as I read the piece that started it all, the exclusive in the *Journal,* and then read all the ancillary coverage. The articles about how I'd stolen from Silicon Valley. How I'd hired others to kill for me. And worst of all, how I'd failed to pull it off.

The *Journal* article discussed at length how the Chinese government neglected to properly test Jiàn's technology. It said the government was "over-eager" and "trying desperately to stay on the forefront" of the bio-economy.

Shame. I'd brought shame on my country. So close to success, I'd been lied to and thwarted again.

This time, it had been in public. I was trapped by the story. There was no turning back, no way to pivot and maneuver and turn this to my advantage.

I looked at the pictures on the *Journal's* website, scrolling past the ones of me and Jiàn headquarters. I stopped at the final photo. It was of Hannah and Lauren Taylor, their insipid blonde heads inclined toward each other, smiling at the camera.

They'd tricked me for the last time. And they'd injured me so greatly, they might think there was no recovering from this. Still, I'd never been one to bother with regret. Action was the only useful remedy for this type of grief.

In one instant, my face, my reputation was shattered. All that remained were shards—but I prided myself on my propensity for reinvention.

I'd find a way to make use of the shards. I'd find a way to make them *bleed*.

CHAPTER 27

HANNAH

Wes rubbed his hands together as the driver maneuvered the car down the freeway and took the exit for Cupertino. We were meeting his real estate agent at the house he'd recently looked at, located about ten miles from Lauren and Gabe's property.

"Wes?"

"Yeah, babe?"

"Are you nervous?"

He bounced his big knee up and down, distractedly looking out the window. "Huh?"

I took that as an answer and peered past him to look at the upscale neighborhood we'd entered. The grand stucco houses had large windows and manicured front lawns. The driver pulled up in front of a particularly large, stunning home. There was no for sale sign out front.

I peered at the mini-mansion. "Is this the right place?"

Wesley smiled. "Yep, this is it. William will meet us here in a minute. He just texted me he's running late."

"It's beautiful."

I'd picked out the house Lauren and I lived in, so I knew a little about the local real estate market—it was *insane*. The modest house we'd grown up in in

Michigan would be worth almost a million dollars in Silicon Valley. This house, in this neighborhood, had to be listed at well over two million dollars. I glanced at Wes. Did he know how much this place cost?

A BMW sedan pulled up behind us a minute later. A compact Hispanic man wearing a three-thousand-dollar suit hopped out, all smiles. William, the real estate agent, clearly knew how much the house cost.

"Wes, Hannah, sorry I'm late. Come on in, Hannah. You're going to love this property. It's turnkey. Immaculate. Wes, I know you already love it."

William ran through the details for my benefit: the house was built in the early nineties, the lot was just under an acre, there was a cul-de-sac at the end of the street. The home was equipped with five bedrooms, four bathrooms, a gourmet kitchen, a solar-heating system, a workout room, and an in-ground pool. "It's perfect for families," William said, beaming at me.

I nodded, unsure of what to make of him, his nonstop smiling, and his suit. He was trying to sell my boyfriend a mansion I wasn't sure he could afford.

At the end of the tour, William brought us back out to the front yard. "So, what do you think?"

"You already know I think it's perfect," Wes said. "Honey? What do you think?"

"It's beautiful. It's in a great neighborhood." I was dying to ask who Wesley needed the five bedrooms for and how on earth he thought he could afford such a place, but I decided to wait.

He studied my face. "Do you love it?"

I looked at the house. "Of course I love it. It's *perfect*."

Wes turned to William. "Make them a full-priced offer. I want it under contract before it goes on the market. Tell them we'll do a short escrow."

William beamed. "Absolutely. I'll call you later." He practically skipped to his BMW and drove off.

Wes smiled first at me, then at the house. "Well, that was easy."

"You can afford this place?" I blurted out.

He looked at me, surprised. "How else did you think I was going to buy it?"

I had no idea what his Betts Security salary was. Used to having plenty of money of my own—my annual salary plus the inheritance from my parents—I'd never given Wesley's financial situation much thought.

"Lauren pays you that much?" I'd always thought my sister was a little reserved with her employee compensation.

"Lauren pays me fairly, within industry standards."

"Fair enough to buy a two-million-dollar-plus home?" I might need to ask my sister for a raise.

His face darkened. "I have money from my parents."

"Oh." I reached out and touched his shoulder. "I didn't know. I'm sorry, I don't mean to make you upset."

"You didn't. I guess we've never really talked about it. We've sort of had a lot of other stuff going on." He held up the key. "William said we can go back in. The owners already relocated, so we're not putting them out. Want to take another look?"

Another smile lit up his face, and I grinned back—his excitement was infectious. "I'd love to."

He held my hand as we went back inside, through the sunny foyer and into the open-concept living room and kitchen. "I love the fireplace," Wes said, going over and running his hands over the marble. "I've always wanted one."

"And that wall is great for a television," I said, pointing to the opposite end of the room. Wes could watch every football game imaginable on an enormous flat-screen TV.

"You're right, but I don't want a television in every room. I want some quiet space, too—I know you love to read."

My heart started racing. He was thinking about me and what I might like to do in his new house? "Huh?"

He looked at me sheepishly. "You need some space to read, right?"

"Y-yeah. That's really nice of you to think of me. But it's going to be *your* house. You can do whatever you want with it."

Wes blew out a deep breath and looked around the room. "But I don't want a house."

"Huh?" I asked again, confused. "Then what are we doing here?"

"I want a home." Wes looked at me, and my heart stopped. "And it would only be a home if you lived here, too."

About to say "huh" for the third time, I forced my mouth shut.

Wes came over and tentatively reached for my hand. "I don't want to pressure you. But…I don't really need a five-bedroom house for just me and all my football trophies and weights."

"You—you don't?"

He arched an eyebrow. "No, I don't."

I bit my lip. "Wes?"

"Yes, baby?"

"What exactly are you asking me?" My voice came out small.

He laughed a little and laced his fingers through mine. "I'm asking you if—once we're both back to normal and feeling settled and ready—you'd like to live here with me. If you would like my home to be your home—*our* home. I want us to live here together forever, or at least until we have so many kids we need a bigger house."

I didn't say anything. I couldn't.

Wes looked worried. "Honey? Am I totally stressing you out? Are you having trouble breathing?"

I started crying.

"Oh shit," he said, clearly panicked. "Do you want to sit down?"

"N-no." My chest was heaving. "Do you mean it? You want to buy this house for *us*?"

"Only if that's a good thing," he said warily.

I threw my arms around his neck and started sobbing. "Yes, it's a good thing. It's the best thing ever."

CHAPTER 28

HANNAH

One Month Later

I yawned and stretched luxuriously across our new king-size bed. Then I remembered what day it was, and I sat up and smiled. "Lauren's bridal shower's today, yay!"

Wes chuckled and rolled over, snuggling with me beneath the blanket. "Do you think *Lauren's* saying yay? Or do you think she's already at the lab, trying to put a few hours in before you subject her to the torture of a silly ritual she has no interest in?"

"Stop it." I smiled.

He went underneath the blanket, sliding down to put his mouth against my belly. "What do you think, huh, little future linebacker? Do you think Auntie Lauren's pissed at Mommy for making her do this?"

I giggled, playing with Wes's hair until he got up to take a shower. We hadn't told anybody, but the sixteen tests I'd taken since skipping my period had confirmed that I'd *never* had the stomach bug. Wes was beside himself with excitement, insisting it was a boy and that he was destined for an illustrious career in the NFL. On the other hand, he thought it might be a girl who would be president of the United States and would have no interest in boys whatsoever until she was thirty.

I'd made no such predictions, still marveling at the life growing inside me, thrilled and terrified and feeling completely blessed. I was too paranoid to share the news yet, even with Lauren. I wanted to wait until we were twelve weeks pregnant, when Dr. Fisher told me the highest risk of miscarriage was past.

Wes thought I was being superstitious, but I still couldn't believe all my good luck. My eyes filled with tears as I lay in the bed, hearing him humming happily to himself in the shower. My cup was running over with happiness.

Not only were we pregnant, we'd moved into our beautiful new house. I was hosting the bridal shower for Lauren later today, and I couldn't wait. Our friends from Paragon were coming, along with Fiona, Bethany, and Gabe's mother. The wedding was next month, and I was beside myself that my sister was *finally* marrying the love of her life.

Biyu and her son had arrived safely at SFO, and had settled rather seamlessly into Silicon Valley life. She started work at Paragon next week, in the computer programming department.

My plans for Li Na had worked better than I ever expected. *The Wall Street Journal* story had gone viral. Li Na's production of the sensor and the gene therapy were halted immediately. The FBI had come through, for once, and pulled off a mass arrest of all Li Na's American contacts, the thugs who'd committed crimes for her. In exchange for lighter sentences, they'd all agreed to provide detailed information about Zhao to the agency, who was actively building a case against her.

Named in both the article and in warrants sought by the FBI, the Chinese government could no longer ignore Li Na's crimes. It finally turned its back on her, stripping Jiàn Innovations of all its licenses and shutting it down. Li Na was to be extradited to the United States, where she would be prosecuted on multiple charges, including trade secret theft, wire fraud, and murder.

Murder. We'd given the name of Jim Pace's killer to the FBI. They were still looking for him, but they had multiple leads. Fiona was thrilled that, finally, steps were being taken to bring her husband's killer to justice.

Justice. It had been too much to hope for, but maybe, just maybe, Li Na Zhao would get hers. I didn't know what her status was, if she was being detained in

China or if they'd begun the extradition process. The FBI had taken over completely, and they wanted us out of it—which was fine by me. For once, I could breathe again, and I was *so* ready to get back to normal.

I rubbed my stomach and grinned. The new normal.

I heard a noise downstairs and called out, "Lauren? Did you come over early to help set up?"

I giggled as I pictured my sister, the center of attention, opening the several packages of sexy lingerie that I'd gotten her from La Perla. She was going to have a fit, and I couldn't wait!

I sat up as I heard another noise. "Lauren?"

But it wasn't Lauren who opened my door. It was Carey, aka Mr. Gray Hoodie, my very expensive snitch.

I clutched the comforter against me. "Carey?"

He smiled when he saw me. It made me feel sick. I opened my mouth to ask what he was doing in my bedroom, but no words came out.

"In here," he called to the person behind him.

I saw a flash of dark hair and opened my mouth to scream, but Carey took out his gun and pointed it at me. "Not a word. Where's the big guy—in there?" We could hear Wes in the shower, still humming.

"Don't." My voice came out a hoarse whisper.

"Shut up." Carey smiled again, heading toward the bathroom as Li Na Zhao stalked into my bedroom.

I stared at her, unbelieving. *Is this a nightmare?*

Carey moved closer to the bathroom.

No, no, no! Time seemed to stop, crawling in slow motion, and it was if my brain couldn't function.

"Wes!" The word came out garbled, as if I were underwater.

Carey undid the safety and hissed at me, "I *said*, shut up!"

"Hannah Taylor, I'd say it's a pleasure to meet you, but I don't have time for lies." She stood at the foot of my bed, her arms crossed against her petite frame.

I jumped out of bed, and she moved in front of me, blocking my path.

Carey went inside the bathroom.

In the slow, stupid grip of my panic, I noticed that Li Na was even more beautiful in person. Her hair was perfect. She wore her signature bright lipstick, a black leather bomber jacket, and slim-fitting pants. *Dressed to kill.*

My heart thudded so hard, I thought it might burst.

"What are you doing here." I couldn't make it sound like a question.

She smiled, playing along, revealing her perfect white teeth. "You ruined my life. And because I have nothing left to lose, I'm here to ruin yours."

The gun went off in the bathroom. I could hear the glass from the shower stall shatter and explode.

Finally finding my voice, I screamed, tears streaming down my face. "*Wes!*"

Li Na at least had the decency to let me finish. Then she stepped forward, her high heels clicking on my hardwood floor. *Who wears high heels to murder someone?* I thought, wildly, but I refused to let that be my last thought—I grabbed my lamp off the nightstand and wielded it, threatening to strike her with it.

I thought of Wes. I thought of our baby, tiny and growing inside me. *Can I reason with her?* "You don't have to do this—"

She took another step forward. "You can't hurt me anymore, Hannah. I'm not afraid of you."

I threw the lamp at her face, but she dodged in time, the impertinent, thieving, murderous c-word of a CEO that she was. She came at me again, but that was when Wes barreled out of the bathroom, stark naked and dripping wet, pointing Carey's gun at her head.

"Wes! Wes." My shoulders shook with sobs as he bolted for us. He shoved the gun against Li Na's head.

She looked at his penis and frowned. "I am not impressed."

He frowned back. "The feeling's mutual."

"Just do it," she snapped, sounding bored. She motioned to the gun. "It's better this way. You get your revenge, I go quick. Win-win."

"Wes—don't. Don't do it!" I shrieked.

Wes looked like he really wanted to do it.

"*Please.* Let her rot in prison like she deserves. Let her wear prison clothes and eat prison food and be somebody's bitch. *Please.*"

Both Li Na and Wes groaned.

But he didn't shoot her.

And he gave me enough time to call the police.

* * *

We'd finished our interviews with the police and the FBI. Carey's body had been removed from the bathroom, and Lauren had hired a service to clean up the rest of the mess.

Li Na had been taken away in handcuffs by Agent Marks, who seemed happy to finally get his hands on her. It turned out she'd bribed several Chinese government officials, managing to escape extradition long enough to get on a private plane to California.

"Can you believe she actually came to your house?" Bethany shivered.

"No. I can't believe it." I took one of the crudités intended for Lauren's botched shower off the tray and unceremoniously stuffed it into my mouth.

Fiona eyed me. "Do you want some wine to go with that? You could probably use it after a day like today."

Lauren, Bethany, and Fiona all leaned forward, waiting for me to finish chewing so I could answer.

"No, thanks," I mumbled. "I'm pregnant."

"I knew it!" Lauren shrieked, hugging me. "Oh my God, I'm going to be an aunt! Pay up," she said to Bethany, who rolled her eyes, but then happily handed over a hundred-dollar bill.

Fiona wiped tears from her eyes and poured wine for the rest of them, while I shoved another appetizer into my mouth. "You did *not* know."

Lauren took a triumphant sip of wine. "Did so. I cannot *wait* for you to have a baby. We're going to play classical music for it, and start math flash cards at an early age, and have a *baby shower* instead of a stupid bridal shower. Okay?"

I giggled. "Okay. I'm not going to say no to you, not today. I'm so sorry about *your* shower."

"I'm not." Lauren grinned, but then her expression turned serious. "Are you *sure* you're okay? Do you think you need to get checked out? That was an awful scare you had."

"I feel fine. But I still don't know why she came here. I mean, I *know* why she came here, but did she really think hurting me and Wes was going to solve her problems?"

Wes, Gabe, Levi, and Ellis came in then. Ash was at FBI headquarters, following up with Agent Marks on behalf of Betts Security. We wanted to make sure we knew *exactly* what was happening with Li Na, unlike earlier today.

Gabe sat down next to Lauren and threw his arm around her. "I don't think she was looking to solve problems per se—I think she was looking for her own version of justice. I think she thought coming after the person who'd shamed her was the only honorable thing to do."

Wes sank down next to me. "I swear, she wanted me to shoot her. She wanted me to end it."

Gabe nodded. "Again, I think that fits with her notion of honor. Rotting in a prison cell isn't very honorable, but going down fighting is."

Ellis stood behind Fiona, while Levi sat near-ish to Bethany, who glared at him.

"What?" he asked. I couldn't tell if he was annoyed by her of if he thought her glaring was cute—maybe both.

She just rolled her eyes.

"I told you Carey was a bad seed." Ellis's voice startled all of us. "You never should've trusted him."

"You're right," I said. "He *did* give me fair warning, though—he said he'd go to the highest bidder. In the end, I guess that was Li Na."

"But Carey served his purpose." Fiona had a sip of wine. "He gave the police the name of Jim's killer."

"True."

Ellis smiled at me, breaking the sad mood. "By the way, congratulations—I can't *wait* to be an uncle."

I grinned at him and then at all my friends. My baby was already the luckiest person I knew.

Later, when everyone had gone home and Wes and I were settled in the guest room, he traced a finger across my jawline.

"That scared the hell out of me today." His eyes were wide, sad.

"Me too. When I heard the gunshot…"

"Shh, don't." He leaned down and nuzzled his face against me. "I Hulk-smashed his ass, and we don't ever have to talk about it again."

"Okay."

We were quiet for a minute, his heart beating against mine. I'd thought he'd fallen asleep when he said, "I was going to wait for the right time for this, the absolutely perfect time, but I'm pretty sure that because we almost died today, and we already bought this house, and we're pregnant, this is it."

"Okay?"

He sat up and reached for the drawer of the nightstand. He pulled out a box and held it out to me shyly.

"What's that?" I knew what it was, but I wanted to hear it.

"Open it."

I opened the box to see the most beautiful ring ever, the exact one I'd circled in all the bridal magazines I'd left lying around the house. It was a large, ethically sourced diamond, mined from sources that followed strict labor regulations and environmental standards.

Hey, when you had specific taste, you needed to be…specific.

"Oh my God! It's gorgeous! It's perfect!"

Wes's eyes sparkled as he slid the ring onto my finger. "I can't imagine spending another day without you. I want to grow old with you, have a family with you, share my life with you. Will you marry me? I love you so much."

I beamed at him. "I love you more. And by the way, the answer is yes. *Hell* yes."

Wes clasped my hand, admiring the way the ring sparkled against my skin. He leaned down and whispered to my stomach, "An ethically sourced, conflict-free engagement ring. Now I've heard everything, little buddy!"

I giggled, then leaned down to kiss the man I loved.

Special Thanks

Thank you to my readers! Every single one of you light up my days. I love hearing from you, and also that you love the Silicon Valley Billionaires…your support means everything!

You can sign up for my mailing list at www.leighjamesbooks.com to be notified of new releases.

Thank you to Marie Force for being an amazing publisher, mentor, and person. Working with you has taught me so much—it's a privilege and an honor! Thanks to the wonderful editing and eagle eye of Linda Ingmanson. Julie Cupp of Jack's House, thank you for always making the publishing process shiny and painless! Also, a huge shout-out to Holly, Lisa, and the team at Jack's House for taking me on and their continued support.

I could not write without the love and support of my husband and my three children. You guys make every day worth it. And a special shout-out to my mom, who is always ready with a pep talk, and who always told me to never give up.

About the Author

Leigh James is an author of contemporary romance and romantic suspense. She is a vocal lover of strapping alpha males in movies, books and real life, which makes her three kids roll their eyes and makes her husband feel appreciated.

When she's not writing, you can usually find her reading or watching Outlander, Game of Thrones, and Vikings (see penchant for alpha males, above). She has a degree in journalism from the University of New Hampshire, which is good for deadlines and word counts, and a law degree from Suffolk University with a Concentration in High Technology Law, which is helpful when writing about sexy tech billionaires with legal woes.

For more information about Leigh, please visit her website *www.leighjamesbooks.com*, "Like" Leigh on Facebook at *www.facebook.com/leighjames19author/* and follow her on Twitter @LeighJames19, Instagram at *www.instagram.com/leighjames_author/* and Goodreads at *www.goodreads.com/author/show/7231254.Leigh_James*. Join Leigh's newsletter at *www.leighjamesbooks.com/form* to be the first to hear about upcoming releases. She's loves hearing from her readers. Email her directly at *leighjames@leighjamesbooks.com*.

CPSIA information can be obtained
at www.ICGtesting.com
Printed in the USA
LVHW02s1524010318
568343LV00011B/892/P